The jungle remained nearly impenetrable, right up to the point where it suddenly thinned out and they stepped onto a grassy verge about ten yards wide. After that, the ground dropped away into the yawning nothingness of the chasm Mariella had spoken of. The Blade of the Gods was a good name for it. Fifty yards wide, evidently hundreds of feet deep, its sides were perfectly sheer and dropped straight down.

Mariella had led them unerringly to the only spot where they could cross the chasm. A four-foot-wide bridge made of thick ropes and rough-hewn planks extended across the giant slash in the earth. Cierra muttered, "Dios mio," when she saw it, and when Gabriel glanced over at her he saw the fear in her eyes. A breeze drifted along the gorge and, at its touch, the bridge swayed back and forth.

They stepped out onto the span, walked cautiously forward. The bridge sagged under their weight. Gabriel saw the ropes attached to the anchor posts tighten around the wood.

This would be a heck of a place for a trap, Gabriel thought.

As if reading his thoughts, Alexei Podnemovitch stepped out of the jungle at the western end of the bridge. He had a gun in his hand. He leveled the revolver at Gabriel. "Not another step, Hunt…"

Enjoy these other Gabriel Hunt adventures:

HUNT THROUGH THE CRADLE OF FEAR *
HUNT AT WORLD'S END *
HUNT BEYOND THE FROZEN FIRE *
HUNT AMONG THE KILLERS OF MEN *
HUNT THROUGH NAPOLEON'S WEB *

* coming soon

GABRIEL HUNT

HUNT
At The Well Of Eternity

AS TOLD TO JAMES REASONER

LEISURE BOOKS NEW YORK CITY

A LEISURE BOOK®

May 2009

Published by

Dorchester Publishing Co., Inc.
200 Madison Avenue
New York, NY 10016

in collaboration with Winterfall LLC

ISBN 10: 0-8439-6246-1
ISBN 13: 978-0-8439-6246-8
E-ISBN: 978-1-4285-0671-8

Visit us on the web at www.dorchesterpub.com or
www.HuntForAdventure.com

HUNT

At The Well
Of Eternity

Chapter 1

Gabriel Hunt tugged at the tight collar around his neck and grimaced as he failed to loosen it. He stuck the thumb of his other hand inside the cummerbund cinched around his waist and pulled it out a little.

"I *hate* tuxedos," he muttered.

His brother Michael leaned closer to him. Without altering the beaming smile on his face, Michael said from the corner of his mouth, "Stop fidgeting."

"Easy for you to say, yours probably fits."

"You could have had one made as well," Michael said. "Thomas would have been delighted. If instead you choose to *rent* from some off-the-rack dealer . . ."

"Best part of wearing a tuxedo's getting to give the damn thing back," Gabriel said. Then he spotted something that interested him more than the collar's constraints.

Some*one*, actually.

The loveliest woman he had seen in quite some time.

She moved toward the Hunt brothers, her natural grace allowing her to glide with apparent ease through the crowd that thronged the Great Hall of the Metropolitan Museum of Art. She was as beautiful as any of the masterpieces hung on the walls in the museum's many galleries.

A mass of midnight-black curls framed a compelling, high-cheekboned face dominated by dark, intense eyes. Those curls tumbled over honey-skinned shoulders left bare by the strapless evening gown of dark green silk that clung to the generous curves of her body. She possessed a timeless, natural beauty that was more attractive to Gabriel than anything the multitude of stick-thin, face-lifted society women attending this reception could ever muster.

And she appeared to be coming straight toward him.

"Who's that?" Gabriel asked his brother.

"I have no idea," Michael replied. "I don't think I've ever seen her before."

"You'd remember if you had," Gabriel said. "I thought you knew everyone here."

Tonight's reception was in honor of a new exhibit of Egyptian art and artifacts, many of which the Hunt Foundation had provided on loan to the museum. Gabriel had brought several of those artifacts back with him from a recent trip to Egypt—some of them even with the knowledge of the Egyptian government. The exhibit would open to the public the next day, but tonight was an advance showing for the museum's wealthiest benefactors.

Gabriel snagged a couple of glasses of champagne from a tray carried by a passing waiter. The beautiful young woman might be thirsty, and if she was, he was going to be ready.

"What's that she's carrying?" Michael asked in an undertone.

It was Gabriel's turn to say, "I have no idea." Instead of some glittery, fashionable purse, the young woman carried a cloth-wrapped bundle of some sort. The cloth was a faded red, and to Gabriel's eye, it appeared old. The fabric looked distressed, the edges frayed.

A waiter moved in front of her, offering her a drink. She shook her head and looked irritated that the man had interrupted her progress across the hall. When Gabriel saw that, he tossed back the champagne in one of the glasses he held, then pressed the other into Michael's hand.

Either the lady didn't drink, or she had something else on her mind at the moment.

Gabriel set the empty glass on a pedestal supporting a clay vase, then turned to greet the young woman with a smile as she finally reached the spot where he and Michael were standing, near one of the pillars that ran along the sides of the hall.

"Señor Hunt?" she said. He caught a hint of a South American accent, but only a hint.

"That's right," Gabriel said, but before he could ask her who she was, she spoke again.

"Señor Michael Hunt?"

Gabriel shot a sidelong glance Michael's way and Michael stepped forward, smiling. Shorter, younger, and studious-looking rather than ruggedly handsome, he was accustomed to paling into insignificance next to his more dynamic older brother. But that didn't mean he had to like it.

"I'm Michael Hunt," he said. "And you are . . . ?"

"My name is Mariella Montez," she told him.

"And what can I do for you, Miss Montez?"

Before she could reply, the waiter who had stopped her on her way across the hall appeared behind her sleek, bare left shoulder. "Excuse me, ma'am, but I believe you dropped this."

With an annoyed look again on her face, she turned

toward the red-jacketed man and said, "I didn't drop anything—"

But what the waiter was extending toward her was a pistol, aimed directly between her ample breasts. He reached out with his other hand to snatch the bundle she was carrying.

Mariella jerked back and said, "No!"

Incredulous and instantly tensed for trouble, Gabriel stepped between Mariella and the waiter. "Hey, buddy, put that thing down. This is a museum, not a firing range."

"This is not your concern," the waiter said, and swung the pistol at Gabriel's head.

Instinct brought Gabriel's left arm up to block the blow. His right fist shot up and out in a short, sharp punch that rocked the waiter's head back and bloodied his nose.

With his now crimson-smeared face contorted with anger, the waiter swung again. This time he slashed at Gabriel's throat. Gabriel leaped backward and collided with the young woman.

Such a collision might have been pleasurable under other circumstances, but not now. Not with a madman of a waiter swinging a gun that he could just as easily start firing at any moment.

Gabriel felt Mariella push him away, then say, "Señor Hunt, you must take this!" But she wasn't talking to him. He heard Michael, behind him, saying, "What is it?" She was probably trying to give Michael the cloth-wrapped bundle, whatever it was. Gabriel didn't have the time to check whether the hand-off had been successful. Instead, he lowered his head and tackled the waiter around the waist, driving the man off his feet. The gun went off as they fell, the bullet shattering a pane of glass in the ceiling twenty feet overhead.

Commotion filled the Great Hall as shards of glass rained down. Some men yelled and pushed forward, demanding to know what was going on. Others scurried out of the way, trampling on the trailing edges of their dates' expensive gowns in their rush to steer clear of the fray. Security guards ran toward the scene of the struggle.

Gabriel knocked the gun out of the waiter's hand, but the waiter darted in under Gabriel's guard, wrapped his fists around Gabriel's throat, and squeezed with a grip like a dockworker's. Gabriel heaved himself off the marble-tiled floor and rolled over in an attempt to break the man's hold. The waiter hung on stubbornly.

Rolling over and then over again, the two men crashed into a pedestal—the same pedestal, in fact, where Gabriel had placed his empty champagne glass a few minutes earlier. It fell to the ground and shattered, spraying shrapnel.

The Egyptian vase that stood on the pedestal was heavier and didn't fall immediately—but Gabriel noted with a surge of concern as it started to topple.

It wasn't fabulously rare or valuable—otherwise it would have been safely behind glass or at least velvet ropes. But it *was* old, and Gabriel watched its growing tilt with alarm.

As the vase tipped over, he let go of the waiter's forearms and shot out a hand to catch it. It landed in his palm, just an inch above the stone floor. One more inch and it would have been a pile of worthless shards, like the shattered window overhead. He lowered it gently.

Meanwhile, though, the waiter had gone on with his attempt to squeeze what little air still remained in Gabriel's lungs out of his body. A red haze was starting to form over Gabriel's vision and rockets were exploding behind his eyes from lack of oxygen. There were people all around them, but no one was reaching in to help—they seemed to be distracted by something else that was going on. Gabriel tried to call out to them, but found himself unable to get a sound out through his constricted throat.

If he hadn't been wearing a goddamn tuxedo, he'd have had his Colt on him and maybe could have gotten to it. Or at least a knife—he'd have had *something*. As it is, he had nothing, except a cummerbund, a bow tie, and maybe a half-minute of consciousness left.

Ah, hell, Gabriel thought. *Dust to dust.*

With a heave, he smashed the vase over the head of the man trying to kill him.

The waiter slumped sideways, and his fingers slipped off Gabriel's throat at last. Compared to their grip, the hated tuxedo collar suddenly felt luxurious. Gasping lungfuls of air, Gabriel sat up. He yanked his bow tie off and ripped his collar stud out, panting.

Then he took stock of the chaos all around him.

The waiter who'd attacked him wasn't the only member of the service staff that seemed to have been overtaken by violent impulses. Several more red-jacketed men had pulled guns from under their jackets and now menaced the crowd, alternating between simply brandishing the weapons and firing them over everyone's head. Smoke from their gunfire hung in the air, stinking of gunpowder and flame. Women screamed, men shouted curses, and vice versa. Everybody was scrambling to get out of the line of fire, though no two people seemed to agree on which direction was safest. As Gabriel leaped to his feet, he saw one man dive into an open stone sarcophagus. Then one of the waiters spotted a security guard leveling a gun at him and without hesitating shot the guard in the chest. Blood sprayed and the crowd screamed.

The gunman swung his automatic toward another guard. Racing up behind him, Gabriel ripped the cummerbund from around his own waist and, holding both ends, dropped it over the gunman's head from behind. He jerked back hard just as the man squeezed the trigger. The shot slammed upward toward the vaulted ceiling and another window high above them splintered.

With the cummerbund forming a makeshift lasso around the gunman's neck, Gabriel swung him face-first into one of the pillars. The crunching impact made the man go limp. Gabriel let go of one end of the cummerbund and allowed the unconscious man to fall to the floor.

Gabriel spun around to look for Michael. He caught a glimpse of his brother and Mariella at the far end of the room, fear-stricken guests dashing back and forth between him and them. Michael had the cloth-wrapped bundle tucked under one arm now, and with his other hand he held the woman's wrist, trying to guide her through the chaos.

More gunshots blasted out, increasing the panic in the room. Gabriel didn't know how many civilians had been hit so far, or whether any had been trampled in the stampede. But it was too optimistic to hope either number was zero.

From the street outside, he heard the sounds of police sirens approaching—but they sounded far away.

He started shouldering his way through the crowd in the direction of Michael and Mariella. He was still several yards away when one of the waiters appeared next to Michael and chopped at his head with a tightly held automatic. The blow landed with a hollow impact that Gabriel could hear even over the din in the vast room. Michael's knees unhinged and he fell, letting go of the woman and dropping the bundle.

"Michael!" Gabriel roared. He fought his way forward.

Mariella screamed as another waiter grabbed her and started dragging her away. She twisted in his grip and punched him, a nice solid right hook. The blow was enough to knock her assailant back a step. She lunged toward the bundle Michael had dropped.

Before she could reach it, a fleeing woman passing by kicked the bundle and sent it rolling across the floor. The cloth unwrapped as it rolled. Gabriel caught a glimpse of the object the cloth had been protecting.

A whiskey bottle.

Mariella threw herself after the bottle, grabbing for it. The waiter who had pistol-whipped Michael was after the bottle, too. He threw people aside to get them out of his way. The automatic rose and fell as he used it to batter a path through the crowd. Mariella was about to snatch the bottle from the floor as the man reached her, grabbed the back of her dress, and hauled her up and shoved her away.

Gabriel finally made it to Michael's side, bent to take hold of his brother's arm and lift him to his feet. Michael was groggy but conscious, a trickle of blood worming down his face from a deep cut in his scalp.

"Can you stand?" Gabriel had to shout to get his attention.

Michael nodded, wincing at the pain the motion must have set off inside his head. Gabriel helped him lean against a pillar and told him to stay there, then headed for Mariella.

The crowd was beginning to thin a little, and Gabriel realized that one purpose of all the shooting had been to herd the throng of guests toward the museum's front entrance, leaving more room for the waiters to go after Mariella. Several bodies lay crumpled on the floor and a few guests crouched cowering in the corners, but much of the high society crowd had already escaped and most of the remaining guests and museum staff were pressing and fighting to get out the doors.

Mariella was just fighting, period. Two more waiters had grabbed her, but they had their hands full holding her while the first one went after the whiskey bottle. She stamped on their feet and kicked at their legs and writhed in their grasp. Before Gabriel could get to her, she tore loose from her captors for a second and tackled the other waiter from behind. As he fell, his hand just missed the bottle he'd been reaching for.

"Get her off me!" the waiter roared to his associates.

The other two men latched on to her again, but by this time Gabriel was there, clubbing his hands together and smashing them into the back of one man's neck. The man went down hard, as if every muscle in his body had gone limp.

Mariella twisted and clawed at the other man's face, leaving red streaks on his cheeks. He threw his hands up as she feinted at his eyes, then she lifted a knee into his groin. He doubled over in agony.

That left only the waiter who was trying to retrieve the bottle, and unfortunately it left him free. He grabbed for it once more.

Mariella cried, "Stop him!" as Gabriel ran past her.

The waiter scooped up the bottle and turned with a satisfied smirk on his face. The expression didn't last long because in the next second Gabriel's fist crashed into his face.

As the man teetered, Gabriel got his first good look at him. He was big, well over six feet tall, with massive shoulders that strained the seams of the uniform jacket. He hadn't gotten those shoulders carrying trays of champagne, nor was waitering likely to be how he'd acquired his broken nose or the network of scars along both cheeks and around his eyes.

The punch had momentum and all of Gabriel's weight and strength behind it. Despite being bigger and heavier than Gabriel, the man reeled from the impact. His hands went up in the air . . .

And the whiskey bottle flew out of his grip, turning over and over as it soared high and then came crashing down to shatter on the marble floor in an explosion of glass and liquid.

Mariella Montez had just seen several men beaten and several more shot, and she'd watched it all without showing any abnormal distress, any grief. But now, as she saw the glass shatter and its contents lost, she screamed, a low, plaintive wail, as if her heart had been ripped out.

Chapter 2

It was such a soul-rending cry that Gabriel had to turn and look at her. She had clapped her hands to her face and her eyes were wide with horror. Before he could ask her for an explanation, Gabriel heard the scuff of shoe leather behind him.

The punch Gabriel landed as he spun would have knocked most men out cold, but not this red-jacketed plug-ugly. The man was still upright, swinging a long, brawny arm in a backhanded swipe that smashed into Gabriel's jaw. Gabriel staggered but managed to stay on his feet.

He yelled, "Michael, no!" as his younger brother came running up and jumped onto the big man's back.

The phony waiter grunted and turned in place with Michael clinging to him, then brushed Michael off like a horse swatting away a fly. As Michael fell backward with his arms windmilling, he crashed into Gabriel. Their legs tangled and both of them went down.

That gave the waiter enough time to grab Mariella, throw her over his shoulder, and start galloping toward one of the rear exits. The other waiters covered his retreat with blazing automatics. Gabriel scrambled up but couldn't give chase. Flying lead forced him to grab Michael and duck behind one of the thick pillars as slugs pitted it.

He risked a glance around the pillar when he heard Mariella scream. She was pounding her fists against her captor's back as he ran, but he didn't seem to feel the blows.

Gabriel grimaced and wished again that he'd brought a gun with him tonight. He would have risked a shot at the son of a bitch's legs to bring him down.

As it was, all he could do was pull his head back while bullets chipped splinters of plaster from the pillar next to his ear. His last sight of Mariella came as she was carried, still struggling, through the rear exit.

"The back!" a cop yelled from the front of the Great Hall. "Somebody cover the back!" Other cops were pouring into the room finally, and Gabriel saw two of them salute, turn on their heels and run out again, no doubt headed for the back.

But they would get there too late, Gabriel knew. Despite all the chaos, the waiters had sliced through the scene with brisk efficiency, like sharks through a school of minnows. Whoever and whatever else they were, they were professionals. Chances were their getaway was already arranged and they would be gone before any of the police could reach the back of the huge museum building.

Gabriel turned to Michael and said, "What the hell were you thinking, jumping on that guy?"

"I had to do something."

"You do plenty," Gabriel said. "Leave the jumping on people to me."

"What was that he was after, anyway? It was rolling and spinning around so much I never got a good look at it."

"I did," Gabriel said. "It was a whiskey bottle."

"A bottle of whiskey!"

Gabriel shook his head. "That's not what I said. Come on."

The shooting had stopped. Police officers and fire department paramedics were spreading out through the hall to check on the people who were injured.

Gabriel frowned as he scanned the room. He didn't see any of the red-jacketed figures they'd taken down during the fray. The phony waiters had taken their wounded with them.

Michael still wasn't too steady on his feet, so Gabriel kept one hand under his brother's arm as he led him toward the spot where the bottle had shattered. He knelt, touched a couple of fingers to the wet spot on the floor, and then smelled them.

"That's not whiskey," he said. Not that he'd thought it had been—whatever had been in the bottle hadn't been dark enough to be whiskey. "Doesn't smell like any other kind of booze, either."

He wet his fingers with the residue again and licked them, causing Michael to exclaim, "For God's sake, Gabriel, don't do that!"

Gabriel looked up. "Why not?"

"It could be some sort of toxin!"

Gabriel waited a moment, then shook his head. "Not a fast-acting one anyway." He tasted it again. "It has no flavor at all." He bent forward, sniffed at the spot directly. "No smell. No color. It's not oily, not viscous. As far as I can tell, it's water. Plain water."

"Some poisons are flavorless and odorless."

Gabriel nodded. "And not oily, sure. But so's water, and I think that's what this was a bottle of."

Michael raised a hand to the cut on his head, winced as he touched it. "Why all that fuss over a whiskey bottle filled with . . . ?"

"Water?"

"They went to a lot of trouble to get it away from Miss Montez."

"Damned if I know."

"You guys freeze!"

The brothers looked up at a beefy NYPD cop with a thick mustache dangling down over his upper lip. He had a service revolver leveled at them.

"Perfect timing, officer," Gabriel said. "If you've got a key to the barn door, feel free to lock it."

"Huh?"

"The horse." Gabriel made a shooing gesture with one hand. "Gone."

The cop turned to Michael. "What's he talkin' about?"

Michael gave Gabriel a look, then said, "Officer, we're not armed, and we didn't have anything to do with what happened here. We were guests at the reception. In fact, our Foundation was cohost of the reception."

The cop nodded toward the pieces of broken glass scattered across the floor. "What's that you were monkeyin' with?"

"That bottle appears to be what the gunmen were trying to obtain," Michael said. "Along with a woman named Mariella Montez, who has been abducted."

"Who's this Montez?"

Gabriel said, "A young woman. About so tall—" Gabriel gestured with one hand. "Black hair. Busty. One of those phony waiters carried her off just before you got here."

The cop sighed wearily. "Oh, Lord. That's kidnappin'.

Means we'll have the damn FBI to deal with, too. Hey, stop that!"

Gabriel had taken a pen from his pocket and was using it to turn one of the larger pieces of broken glass over. "Look," he said to Michael. "Most of the label is still intact."

Michael leaned over and put his hands on his knees, squinting to study the label. The cop bent over beside him. "Old Pinebark," Michael read. "Brewed in . . . Dobie's Mill, Florida." He looked at Gabriel and shook his head. "I've never heard of it."

"That doesn't exactly surprise me, Michael," Gabriel said as he straightened. "But I haven't either. And here I thought I'd sampled just about every brand of rotgut, hooch, and Who-hit-John under the sun."

"That's hardly something to boast about," Michael muttered.

"How about you, officer? You ever hear of Old—" But looking up, Gabriel saw the policeman wasn't listening. He was staring at the cloth that had been wrapped around the bottle. It was lying on the floor of the Great Hall, wadded up and soiled from being trampled underfoot.

Gabriel walked over to it, squatted down on his haunches. There was some sort of design on the cloth. He used the tip of his pen to straighten it out.

"There you go, messing with evidence again," the cop complained.

The cloth was perhaps thirty inches square. The faded colors and some tattering around the edges indicated that it was quite old; there were long-dried bloodstains spattered along one edge and even a dark-rimmed bullet hole in one spot. Crossed sabers were emblazoned in each corner. Set in a large, gilt-edged circle that took up most of the center of the flag was a picture of a gray-uniformed man on a magnificent, rearing stallion. In the background was a large white house with white columns, set among rolling green hills and fields covered with lush crops. Letters that arched above the circle read *Fifth GA. CAVALRY*, and below the picture, set slightly apart, were the letters *C S A*.

Gabriel said, "You're the one with the history degree. Want to tell me what we're looking at?"

"It appears," Michael said, "to be the battle flag of a Confederate cavalry regiment."

"The Fifth Georgia Cavalry was commanded by Brigadier General Granville Fordham Fargo," Michael said several hours later as he pointed at a yellowed page in the over-sized volume spread open on the room's cherrywood reading table, itself an antique. He and Gabriel were in the Sutton Place brownstone that served as the headquarters of the Hunt Foundation, as well as Michael's home.

The brothers had spent a portion of the intervening hours being questioned by the police at the scene, but they hadn't been able to tell the cops anything beyond what was obvious: Someone had substituted gunmen for the real waiters who were supposed to serve at the reception, apparently for the purpose of kidnapping Mariella Montez and stealing the bottle she had brought with her to the museum. When the bottle shattered, they satisfied themselves with just grabbing her.

The grisly discovery of the bodies of the real waiters in the catering van parked behind the museum provided grim confirmation. Each of them had been killed by a single shot to the back of the head. Professional executions.

Instead of returning to his own rooms on the top floor

of the Discoverers League building, Gabriel had come here to the brownstone with Michael. Michael had been sorting through one musty volume after another in the library adjoining his office for over an hour while Gabriel paced impatiently. The books Michael had pulled from the shelves were stacked in neat piles on the floor and the table. Only two were open.

Gabriel reversed a chair and straddled it as Michael went on, "The Fifth Georgia was raised from a county in the southern part of the state, near the border with Florida. Just across the border is where this place Dobie's Mill was located. That also happens to be the location of the only major battle the regiment took part in, the Battle of Olustee. That was in 1864. There's a list here of all the officers who served."

"I don't guess any of them were named Montez?"

Michael shook his head. "No."

"What about that Old Pinebark distillery? You find anything about that?"

Michael hesitated. He loosened his bow tie and pulled it from around his neck, then opened his collar, which he hadn't done until now. Gabriel had long since thrown his tuxedo jacket over the back of a chair, with the tie and cummerbund stuffed in the pockets.

"That's actually rather odd," Michael said. He moved over to the second open book, turned it around so it was facing Gabriel. "According to Hogan's *History of Distilling in America*, the Old Pinebark distillery was destroyed during the war and never rebuilt."

"I don't suppose you mean World War II," Gabriel said.

"No," Michael said. "The Civil War."

Gabriel frowned. "That would mean that bottle was at least—"

"A hundred forty-four years old," Michael said with a nod.

"So we've got an antique whiskey bottle wrapped in a battle flag from the Civil War," Gabriel said.

"Yes, and if the police find out that we have them, we're going to be in trouble," Michael warned.

The cop who had questioned them at the museum had been called away by one of his superiors, and Gabriel had taken the opportunity to carry the flag over behind one of the pillars, where he quickly folded it up and stashed it at the small of his back, under his shirt. The piece of broken glass with the label attached had gone into his pocket.

The flag was now spread out on the table next to the books. The piece of the bottle rested atop the elaborately decorated cloth.

"What did you find out about Mariella Montez?"

"Nothing," Michael said. He waved in the direction of the computer sitting in one corner of the room, as out of place among the ceiling-high shelves of old books as a cell phone in a monastery. "Not even online. It's as if . . . she doesn't exist."

"She exists, all right," Gabriel said, thinking about the way Mariella had felt to him when he bumped into her. Though he'd been too distracted to appreciate it at the time, he wouldn't soon forget that steel-under-velvet body.

Gabriel went on, "Why'd she want to give the flag and the bottle to you?"

Michael spread his hands. "Lots of people bring antiques to the Hunt Foundation—to evaluate, to identify. To buy. Usually items of older vintage than the Civil War, true, but . . ."

"You think she wanted you to buy them from her?" Gabriel asked. "An old whiskey bottle full of water?"

"It may have had some sort of value other than the

purely economic," Michael said, and Gabriel remembered how she'd screamed when the bottle broke.

"There's one way to find out," Gabriel said.

"How?"

"You said the distillery was in northern Florida, near where this regiment fought its only battle . . . ?"

"That's right," Michael said. "Olustee."

"Then it looks like I'm going to Florida," Gabriel said.

Chapter 3

Gabriel figured it was best to get out of New York as quickly as possible, and Michael knew better than to try to talk him out of it.

Taking the flag and the bottle fragment with him, Gabriel made a quick stop at the Discoverers League to change out of the tuxedo and throw a few things in a bag. He was accustomed to traveling light.

The heaviest thing he put in the bag was his old Colt .45 double-action Peacemaker with well-worn walnut grips. Legend had it that the gun had once belonged to a notorious Western shootist, although the owner changed from Billy the Kid to Bat Masterson to Wyatt Earp depending on which Old West expert you talked to.

Gabriel didn't know if any of the stories were true. All he cared about was that the revolver was a fine old weapon in top-notch shape, and that it packed plenty of stopping power.

Wearing a broken-in brown leather bomber jacket against the late-night chill along with brown boots, khakis, and a dark blue work shirt, Gabriel threw his bag into the backseat of the convertible he kept in the League's garage and headed for the small private airfield on Long Island where several aircraft belonging to the Hunt Foundation were hangered. It was well after midnight by now, but there was still a considerable amount of traffic on the Queensboro Bridge.

Not so much, though, that Gabriel didn't notice the headlights coming up fast behind him as he made the turn onto the on-ramp.

His right foot increased its pressure on the accelerator. The convertible didn't look like anything special, but Gabriel had souped up the engine so that it responded with a smooth, powerful purr and shot ahead.

At the same time, keeping his right hand on the wheel, he reached into his jacket with his left hand and pulled a cell phone from his shirt pocket. He didn't have to look to see what he was doing as he flipped it open and thumbed a speed-dial number.

"Michael," he said into the phone when his brother answered, "lock the brownstone down now."

"Gabriel?" Michael's voice sounded fuzzy, as if the phone call had dragged him out of sleep. "What's wrong?"

"Just get the place locked down, then I'll tell you."

"Are you in trouble again?"

The fast-moving headlights behind him had cut the gap between the cars by a considerable margin, and Gabriel wasn't halfway across the bridge yet. He weaved around a van and heard tires screeching and brakes squealing behind him. His pursuers were taking chances, trying to catch up to him before he reached the other end of the bridge. They probably hoped to force him off into the East River.

"No more than usual," Gabriel said.

"Damn it," Michael said. "Hang on." Gabriel heard some shuffling on the other end, then the triple beep of the security system being activated. "All right," Michael said a second later. "I'm locked in. Now, what can I do to help you?"

"Nothing."

"Where are you?"

"Queensboro Bridge." Gabriel sped up even more, but the headlights were gaining on him. The vehicle, a big black SUV, loomed behind him and rammed into the convertible's rear end with a bone-jarring jolt. The car skidded toward the railing, high above the river, but Gabriel coolly steered out of the skid and regained control. "Somebody's trying to keep me from leaving town."

"My God! Are you all—"

"I'm fine, but I've got to go. Stay inside until you hear from me. Have your guys check all deliveries, even food."

Michael started to say something else, but Gabriel was already flipping the phone shut. He stowed it away in his pocket and got both hands on the wheel again just as the SUV pulled up on the convertible's right rear corner. It rammed hard into the fender and sent the smaller vehicle into a spin.

The other drivers on the bridge had seen that something was wrong and had pulled out of the way of the speeding cars. Which was good in terms of reducing the odds that he'd hit anyone, but it also meant there was nothing to stop his spin. He kept his left hand on the wheel, for what little good it did, and reached into the backseat with his right. He'd left the top of his bag unzipped, and his fingers wrapped around the butt of the Colt.

He jerked the gun free as the car slid to a stop across two lanes, facing the lights of Roosevelt Island. The driver's side was pointing toward the SUV, which had braked sharply after the collision. It picked up speed now, though, and Gabriel realized that the driver was planning to T-bone the convertible.

Gabriel tried cranking the ignition, but the convertible's engine had died. He shifted the revolver from his right hand to his left and thrust it out the window. He leveled the Colt at the oncoming SUV and squeezed off three rounds as he continued twisting the key in the ignition with his other hand.

All three slugs smacked into the SUV's windshield, but they just starred the glass and didn't even come close to shattering it. Still trying to start the car, Gabriel lowered his aim and put two shots into the SUV's grille. That didn't do any good, either. The damn thing had to be armored.

Just about what you would expect from professionals like the men who had raided the museum.

The engine finally caught. Gabriel slammed the convertible into reverse. Smoke rose from the tires as the car peeled backward. The SUV was practically on top of it already and clipped the front bumper as it rocketed past.

Gabriel dropped the Colt on the seat beside him and kept backing, twisting the wheel as he did so.

Now he was behind the SUV, which had screeched to a stop inches from the railing. He floored the accelerator and started crowding the other car's right rear. Sparks flew in the night as metal clashed. The SUV's rear end slewed to the left and clipped the railing. It began to drag against the metal beams. He considerer ramming the SUV, trying to push it off into the water, but the convertible was considerably lighter than the other vehicle—it wasn't likely to work. And anyway, Gabriel had a plane to catch.

Gabriel whipped the wheel to the right and cut across several lanes. He kept the gas pedal pushed down as far as it would go and shot down the slope to the foot of the bridge.

The darkness of Queens Bridge Park loomed to his left. He sent the convertible skidding into a left turn on Vernon Boulevard and then almost immediately turned right on a smaller street. No lights appeared in his rearview mirror. Evidently the men who'd been trying to kill him weren't prepared to follow him through the side streets of Queens.

He kept making turns for several minutes, just to throw off any possible pursuit, then cut back south toward the Long Island Expressway. His nerves were steady despite the attempt on his life. It wasn't his first. But he heaved a sigh of relief anyway.

Then he reached for his cell phone.

"Everything's quiet here," Michael said. "Are you okay?"

"Just annoyed. Oh, and the convertible took some damage. I'll leave it at the airfield and you can have somebody pick it up tomorrow."

"Of course. What happened?"

"Somebody in an SUV just tried to push me off the Queensboro Bridge. Our friends from earlier in the evening, I'd guess."

"How did they find you?"

Gabriel felt a pang of anxiety for Mariella. "I'm guessing they forced Señorita Montez to tell them who she was trying to give her package to. That's why I told you to lock everything down at the brownstone. If they found me, they can find you."

"Well, they can find me," Michael said, "but no one's getting in without my say-so."

"Good," Gabriel said. "Don't give it to any men in a black SUV."

"Or any waiters," Michael said.

Gabriel grinned as he drove through the night. "That's right. Or any waiters." He shut the phone off. The airstrip was near.

Michael had shown him on a map where the Battle of Olustee had been fought in 1864. The nearest town with an airport was St. Augustine, "the oldest European settlement on the North American continent," the guidebook entry Gabriel had consulted said, "founded by Spanish explorers more than five hundred years ago." He had called ahead to have the Foundation's private jet readied for takeoff, so as soon as he'd filed a flight plan for St. Augustine, Gabriel got in the air.

When he was at cruising altitude and had switched the autopilot on, he was finally able to sit back and think about everything that had happened over the past several hours. He had certainly never expected so much excitement when he'd struggled into that monkey suit for the reception at the museum. At most he had thought that he might find some willing female companionship for a late supper and a few drinks after the reception, followed by . . .

Well, things hadn't gotten anywhere near that far, Gabriel reflected. The most attractive woman he had met tonight was Mariella Montez, and their relationship had been brief, hectic, and filled with mystery and danger.

Not the worst start to an evening, Gabriel reflected, but the ending could've been better. No man likes seeing his prospective date carried off by a linebacker in livery.

He had no idea where Mariella was and preferred not to think too much about what was happening to her. The men who had carried her off were clearly the sort to stop at nothing to get what they wanted.

And what, exactly, was that? A tattered battle flag and an antique whiskey bottle? What made those two items so special?

The flag and the piece of the bottle were in Gabriel's bag. He went back into the jet's passenger cabin, leaving the plane to fly itself, and got them out to study them. He looked at the bottle first.

There was nothing special about it that he could see. The printing on the label had faded with time, of course, but it was all still legible. He could still make out the two pine trees that flanked the name OLD PINEBARK. He turned the piece of glass over and peered through it at the back of the label, just in case something had been written or drawn on it before it was pasted on the bottle.

Nothing.

He set the piece aside and unfolded the flag, spreading it out on a table under a good light. The picture in the center of the flag had a lot of detail worked into it. Behind the cavalryman on the rearing horse was a large field of some sort.

A cotton field, of course. There were even tiny figures in the field. Slaves. Gabriel's mouth tightened.

More men on horseback galloped over the hills to the right of the figure in the foreground, near the bullet hole. A hunt, perhaps? To the left was the plantation house, with more tiny figures in front of it. Southern belles in hoop skirts. It was like a scene out of *Gone With the Wind*.

He sat down in one of the cushioned seats around the table and leaned back. How had these artifacts of the Old South wound up in the hands of the beautiful young woman who had brought them to the Metropolitan Museum to give to Michael Hunt?

He didn't have an answer. And he had no idea if any

answers would be waiting for him in Florida. It was just the only place he had to start looking.

Gabriel stared at the flag until his eyes hurt, feeling like there was something there he wasn't seeing. After a while he shook his head and gave up. It might be better to come back to it later, he decided, and study the situation with fresher eyes . . . and a fresher brain, to boot. It had been a long night and he hadn't had any sleep so far, not to mention having to fight for his life several times. And he still had miles to go.

Florida loomed up ahead in the darkness as he returned to the cockpit and the jet continued to arrow southward. The Sunshine State.

Maybe it would shine some light on the ugly mystery that had already cost a dozen people their lives.

Chapter 4

Gabriel rented a car at the St. Augustine airport, then found a motel room not far away and crawled into bed for a few hours of much-needed sleep. When he got up the next morning his muscles were a little sore from the battering they had taken the night before, but the stiffness went away after a half hour in the motel's pool.

Over breakfast in the motel coffee shop he studied a map he had taken from a rack in the office that showed how to get to the Olustee battlefield and historical site. As the waitress paused by his table to freshen his coffee, she said, "You goin' out to the battlefield, hon?"

Gabriel smiled. "That's right."

"That's funny, you don't look like a Civil War buff."

"Get a lot of them through here, do you?"

"Oh, yeah, those reenactors come down to the battle-field all the time. You know, they've filmed some Hollywood movies there, durin' the reenactments those fellas put on."

"No, I didn't know that," Gabriel said. Since the woman was talkative and the coffee shop wasn't very busy, he asked her another question. "I suppose there are descendants of men who fought in the battle living around here?"

"Sure. Most of the fellas in the battle were Florida boys. On the Confederate side, anyway."

"What about General Fargo? Any of his descendants in these parts?"

The woman frowned. "Who?"

"General Granville Fordham Fargo. He commanded a cavalry regiment during the battle."

The waitress shook her head. "Sorry. I don't know anybody named Fargo who lives around here. And I've been in St. Augustine all my life."

"Well, it was a Georgia cavalry regiment," Gabriel said.

"There you go. The general and his boys must've gone back home. Those that were lucky enough to make it home." The woman leaned over the table and tapped a finger on the map. "You know you're not gonna be able to get out there today, right?"

Gabriel shook his head and said, "No, I didn't know that. Why not?"

"Road's washed out. We had a tropical storm come through here last week, and all the damage hasn't been repaired yet. Only way in is through the creeks and the sloughs and the swamps."

That didn't sound very promising. Gabriel had slogged through more than one swamp in his life. He didn't like them. Didn't like the mud, and the roots that wrapped around a man's ankles, and the cottonmouths and the gators and the mosquitoes that sometimes seemed damned near big enough to carry you off.

But he hadn't come to Florida to sit around a motel waiting for a road to be repaired.

"Any place around here I can rent a boat?"

"You'll need an airboat to get where you want to go."

"What about a place I can rent an airboat, then?"

"Just so happens you're lucky today, hon." The waitress pointed to a man sitting at the counter. "There's the fella you'd need to talk to, right there." She raised her voice. "Hey, Hoyt!"

The man looked up. "Yep?"

The waitress motioned to him. "Come over here. This fella wants to go out to the battlefield."

Gabriel would have preferred not to have his business announced to the entire coffee shop, but it was too late to worry about that now. Hoyt got up from the stool at the counter and came over to the booth Gabriel occupied, taking his time about it. He carried his coffee cup in his left hand.

He was somewhere in his sixties, Gabriel estimated, although with a man who had obviously spent much of his life outdoors it was hard to tell his age. Hoyt was short and slender, with a lined, leathery face and a short gray beard. He wore a Jacksonville Jaguars cap, a work shirt with the sleeves rolled up over deeply tanned forearms, and faded jeans.

"You don't look like one o' those reenactors," Hoyt commented as he came up to the table.

"I'm not," Gabriel said. He put out his hand. "Gabriel Hunt."

"Hoyt Johnson." He shook Gabriel's hand.

"I gather you have an airboat."

"Sure do. Make my livin' guidin' huntin' and fishin' parties. You much of an angler?"

"When I get the chance," Gabriel said. He motioned to the bench seat on the other side of the table. "Why don't you sit down and join me?"

"Don't mind if I do." Hoyt slid into the seat and held out his cup to the waitress, who still stood there with the coffee. "Hot that up a little, would you, Patsy?"

When they both had fresh coffee and the waitress had gone back behind the counter, he asked, "You're not a drug smuggler, are you?"

"What? No, of course not."

"It's just that you look like a fella who knows his way around. Not the touristy type, if you get my drift."

"I *am* here on business," Gabriel admitted.

"Not illegal business?"

The only crime he'd committed lately was tampering with evidence. Well, that and discharging a firearm illegally on the Queensboro Bridge. But he didn't think the men in the SUV would be filing any complaints with the police about the incident.

"No," Gabriel said with a shake of his head.

"Well, you don't look any more like a crook than you do a Civil War buff, I guess," Hoyt said. "I can take you out there to the battlefield. Not today, though. Have to be tomorrow."

Gabriel didn't want to wait. For one thing, that would give the men who wanted him dead more time to figure out where he had gone.

"It's worth some extra money to me to go out there today," Gabriel said.

"How much more extra?"

"I suppose that's for you to decide."

"Well . . . I'll take you out there and back for three hundred bucks."

Gabriel had a feeling that Hoyt would be disappointed—maybe even suspicious—if he agreed to the price right away. So even though Gabriel could have paid double without hesitation he said, "How about two hundred?"

Hoyt appeared to think it over, then said, "Split the difference?"

"Done," Gabriel said and extended his hand again. The two men shook on the deal.

"When were you wantin' to leave?" Hoyt asked.

"As soon as I finish breakfast."

Hoyt pointed out the window. "Go right down this road half a mile and you'll come to the marina where I keep my boat. I'll go gas her up and see you in a little while."

The old-timer left the coffee shop. Gabriel finished his eggs and toast, drained his coffee mug, thanked the waitress for her help, and went out to the rental car. He didn't need to go back to his room for anything. The Colt was already tucked behind his belt at the small of his back, concealed by the bomber jacket. Until this mess was settled, he didn't intend to go unarmed any more often than he had to.

He saw a sign pointing the way to Ponce de Leon Harbor and remembered reading that St. Augustine, in addition to being the oldest settlement on the continent, was also supposed to be the home of the legendary Fountain of Youth. Probably a lot more tourists came here because of that than did to see some Civil War battlefield, Gabriel reflected. But at least the battlefield you could see. Good luck renting a boat to take you to the Fountain of Youth.

A number of airboats were docked at the marina Hoyt had mentioned. The giant fans that propelled them were mounted at the rear of the boats, which were little more than rafts with seats attached to them. Gabriel spotted Hoyt on one of the boats, and the old-timer waved when he saw Gabriel coming along the dock.

"Come aboard," Hoyt called.

Gabriel stepped from the dock onto the boat. Hoyt waved him into one of the seats.

"Ready to go?" he asked as he stood beside the motor.

Gabriel nodded. "Any time you are."

Hoyt cast off the line that held the boat to the dock, then pulled the motor's start rope a couple of times. The motor caught on the second pull. The giant fan was just a blur as the motor's roar rose into the air above the marina. The boat eased away from the dock and out into the harbor, where Hoyt turned it toward an inlet and increased the throttle. The boat began to skim over the water.

Hoyt steered it skillfully into a wide watercourse that separated a narrow island from the mainland, then veered off into a smaller channel. Over the noise of the motor he called to Gabriel, "There's so many rivers, creeks, and sloughs once you get inland that a fella's got to know where he's goin' or he's liable to wander around for days out there!"

Gabriel nodded, the wind of their passage ruffling his hair. "I've been in swamp country before," he shouted back. "I know what it's like."

They soon left St. Augustine behind them. Penetrating the interior of northern Florida was hardly like venturing into the jungles of South America or Africa, but it really didn't take long to reach an area where there were a lot fewer signs of civilization. Great pine forests crowded against the stream banks in places, while in others the channel wound through mangrove swamps. The airboat glided past an occasional peanut field and vast expanses of saw grass.

They were cutting across country, avoiding the sprawling metropolis of Jacksonville, but there were still planes flying overhead and power line towers jutting up into the blue sky. When you kept your eye on the water and the surrounding landscape, though, with fish jumping and flamingos standing around mangrove roots and moss hanging from the trees, it was easy to see that some things hadn't changed much over the years. Much of this territory looked the same as it had when Seminole Indians paddled dugouts along these same creeks and sloughs.

"How long will it take us to get there?" Gabriel asked.

"Be about an hour!" Hoyt replied.

Gabriel sat back. He didn't know if he would find what he was looking for at the battlefield. He wasn't even sure just what he was looking for. He'd know it if he found it. And if he didn't find anything, he'd know that, too. In that case he'd have to find some other place to pick up the trail.

The one thing he wouldn't do was to entertain any notions of failure. He would find Mariella Montez, and he would find out what was behind her kidnapping and the attack at the museum, and he wouldn't stop looking until he did.

Splinters suddenly jumped from the wooden armrest of his seat. Gabriel stared at the raw place on the armrest for half a second before he realized that a bullet had done the damage. He jerked around to look behind them. The fan blades were moving so fast that it seemed unlikely a bullet could have made it through them.

"What's wrong?" Hoyt shouted.

Before Gabriel could answer, a bullet struck the outboard motor's housing, whining off into the hot and sticky air. Hoyt jumped. "Son of a bitch!"

Twisting in his seat, Gabriel saw that another airboat had emerged from the mouth of a slough they had just passed. The tall saw grass had hidden it until now. It surged across the water after them, and the man standing on its bow with a rifle in his hands brought the weapon to his shoulder and leveled it.

"Get down!" Gabriel shouted.

The old-timer flung himself against the tiller and sent the boat slicing to the side in such a sharp turn that Gabriel thought for a second it was going to overturn. He looked back and saw that the rifleman had lowered the gun. Now he was urging the man at the controls to go faster.

"Can you lose them?" Gabriel shouted at Hoyt.

"Damn sure try!" the old-timer replied. He increased the throttle until the airboat was going so fast Gabriel felt like it might leave the water at any time.

The other airboat fell behind for a moment but then increased its speed as well. Gabriel didn't want to try firing his Colt through the fan because the bullets might bounce back from the blades. Anyway, the range was a little too much for a handgun.

Not for a rifle, though. Gabriel heard ringing sounds as bullets panged off the fan blades. If it was hit enough times it might be damaged and stop running. Then the other airboat could overhaul them with no trouble and he and Hoyt would be sitting ducks for the rifleman.

The bad guys had gotten out here in the swamp in a hurry. Gabriel wondered if a member of the gang had been in the coffee shop, keeping an eye on him, and had heard the waitress announce that he was going out to the Olustee battlefield.

With a huge spray of water, the airboat turned from the channel it had been in and began weaving through some mangroves. Gabriel's jaw tightened. He thought that at any second one of the underwater roots might rip the bottom out of the airboat or flip it into the air, but Hoyt seemed to know where he was going.

"This ought to throw 'em off our trail," he called to Gabriel. He didn't appear to be all that flustered by being shot at, and Gabriel wondered just what sort of things the old swamp rat had been mixed up with in the past.

The boat emerged into another long channel between fields of saw grass. It was empty in both directions as far as Gabriel could see. Hoyt turned to the right, proceeding at a less breakneck pace now.

They hadn't gone a hundred yards when, with a roar, the other airboat surged out into the channel behind them.

"Son of a gun!" Hoyt exclaimed. "That fella must have a pretty good man at the tiller to get through those mangroves." The airboat jumped ahead again as he goosed the motor. He looked back at Gabriel. "Don't you worry. I know a place where we can lose 'em for sure!"

"You'd better find it fast," Gabriel said, pointing. A couple of men on Jet Skis had appeared in the channel in front of them and were racing toward the airboat, firing guns as they came.

Chapter 5

At least he had some suitable targets for the Colt now. Gabriel reached behind his back and whipped out the revolver. He leveled it and squeezed off two shots at the man on the right as Hoyt shouted, "Give 'em hell!"

The man Gabriel had targeted went backward off the Jet Ski, which shot into the air as it went out of control. The other man veered away as Gabriel swung the Colt toward him. Gabriel triggered one shot but then held his fire as the man circled and retreated.

"Son of a—" Hoyt exclaimed. Gabriel jerked his head and saw that smoke was coming from the airboat's motor now. Hoyt shouted, "Bullet must'a nicked an oil line! We can't keep runnin' full out like this!"

"Can you fix it?" Gabriel asked.

"Yeah, if folks'll quit shootin' at us!"

Gabriel thought for a second. "You ever play chicken?"

"Now you're talkin'!" Hoyt said as a grin creased his leathery face.

His hands moved with assurance on the controls. The airboat wheeled to the left—to port, Gabriel corrected himself; this was a boat, after all—and kept turning until it was headed straight back at the airboat that had been pursuing them.

"Get behind the seats!" Gabriel called to Hoyt. That meager cover probably wouldn't stop a high-powered rifle bullet, but it was better than no cover at all.

He had extra bullets in a pocket. He stretched out on his belly on the bottom of the airboat and thumbed fresh rounds into the Colt's cylinder, loading all six chambers.

The other airboat wasn't backing off. The two craft leaped at each other, the gap between them closing in a matter of heartbeats as the men at the controls held both throttles wide open.

Gabriel braced his gun hand with the other hand around his wrist and began firing. He felt the wind-rip of a bullet near his head but didn't hear it because the roar of the airboat's motor drowned out the slug's whine.

The rifleman had bellied down, too, to make himself a smaller target. As the airboats roared toward each other, the space between them narrowed to the point that Gabriel could make out the man's face. It was no surprise that he recognized it.

The rifleman was the ugly bastard who had carried Mariella Montez out of the Metropolitan Museum of Art.

"Who's gonna blink?" Hoyt called. Black smoke continued to trail behind the motor, but so far it hadn't missed a beat.

"Better be them," Gabriel said. The other airboat loomed in front of them, mere feet away. If neither pilot's nerve broke, this was going to be one hell of a crash.

But then the other airboat suddenly juked to the left as the man at its controls shoved the tiller over. Hoyt's boat shot past so close that Gabriel almost expected the two vessels to scrape against each other. He twisted his neck to look behind them and saw that the other boat had turned so sharply that it left the water entirely, soaring several feet into the air and tipping to the side. The rifleman and the pilot both had to leap for their lives as the boat went over.

The out-of-control airboat was almost upside down as it slammed into the water with a huge splash and broke apart. The fan was still whirling madly and stirred up the water even more in the second or two before the motor stopped. With all the silvery spray in the air, Gabriel lost sight of the two men.

He said to Hoyt, "Get us out of here and find a quiet place where you can repair that engine."

"Sure thing. I think I'm gonna have to charge you the whole three hundred, though."

"We had a deal," Gabriel said with a grin.

"I charge extra for gettin' shot at."

"Fair enough," Gabriel said.

Hoyt found a shady slough where the thick, overhanging mangrove limbs gave them some concealment in case anybody else came looking for them. While Gabriel swatted at mosquitoes and watched snakes wriggling past in the water, Hoyt repaired the oil line.

When Hoyt was done, he slapped the engine housing and said, "We're ready to go. You still want to head for the battlefield?"

"That's right," Gabriel said. "Why wouldn't I?"

"Well, it seems to me that those fellas with the guns didn't want you goin' out there."

"I don't let little things like that stop me."

Hoyt chuckled. "I didn't really figure you would. Just thought I'd ask."

It was quiet and peaceful under the mangroves, but Gabriel was glad to get moving again. The wind kept the mosquitoes off and cooled him down some. His shirt was dark with sweat.

About thirty minutes later Hoyt brought the airboat to a stop next to a dock that extended a short distance into the stream they had been following. An asphalt road started at the dock and led off through a thick stand of pines.

"Battlefield's a couple hundred yards that way," Hoyt said, pointing up the road. "Want me to come with you?"

"That shouldn't be necessary," Gabriel said. He stepped from the boat up to the dock.

"I'll tinker with this motor some more, then. Make sure the repair job I did will hold up until we get back."

Gabriel walked along the road until it merged with another road leading from the highway. This was the road the tropical storm had washed out, he assumed. To his left was the battlefield site's parking area, and just beyond it the visitor center and museum. Behind the visitor center Gabriel could see a long open field bordered by swamp on one side and a pine forest so thick as to almost be impenetrable on the other. That was the battlefield itself, he supposed.

This was a state park, he reminded himself, so it was probably illegal for him to be carrying his Colt. But he figured breaking the law was the lesser of evils when people were out to kill him.

With the road closed and few, if any, tourists arriving by airboat, he knew the visitor center might be closed, in which case the trip out here could well have been for nothing. But he had come this far and wasn't going to turn back now. He walked on toward the building.

A man pushed open the glass door and stepped out as Gabriel approached. The man was wearing a butternut-colored Confederate army uniform, complete with a campaign cap and brown pack. He carried a long muzzle-loading rifle with a bayonet attached to the barrel. With no one in modern dress around other than Gabriel himself, it felt a little like stepping back in time.

Then he heard a ringing noise and the Confederate soldier took a cell phone out of his pocket and answered it. So much for time travel.

By the time Gabriel reached him, the man had finished his conversation and was putting the phone away. He was wearing modern wire-framed glasses, too, Gabriel noted, instead of old-fashioned spectacles. He said, "Sorry, sir, we're closed today. Most of the staff and volunteers can't get in because of problems with the road."

"You're here," Gabriel pointed out. "Or have you, ah, been here since the battle?"

The man looked puzzled for a second, then laughed. "You mean the uniform? I'm one of the reenactors here. I was just trying on a new uniform when I saw you walking up the road. Did you come by airboat?"

"That's right."

"I suppose I could let you take a look around, since you went to that much trouble. I'm Stephen Krakowski, by the way."

"Gabriel Hunt." Gabriel shook hands with the man.

"Come on inside." Krakowski led Gabriel into the visitors center, which had the usual exhibit cases, gift shop, and snack bar that most such tourist attractions sported. "Are you interested in the Battle of Olustee in particular, or the Civil War in general?"

"I'm interested in this battle," Gabriel said as he headed for the glass display cases. In one, he saw there were flags spread out. "One cavalry regiment in particular." He studied the flags, looking for a match to the one Mariella Montez had brought to New York. He didn't see one.

"Which regiment?"

"The Fifth Georgia."

"Ah. General Fargo's regiment."

Gabriel tried to keep from looking too eager. "You're familiar with it?"

"Of course. I even played General Fargo in a re-enactment one time." Krakowski leaned the rifle he'd been carrying against the display case, then went into the gift shop and came back with an oversized leatherbound book. "This isn't for sale, but we keep it on hand for reference. The local historical society had it printed up around the turn of the century."

"You mean the turn of the twentieth."

"Of course." Krakowski set the volume on one of the display cases and opened it. "This is a history of the battle put together from the accounts of several officers who participated in it. It lists all the units and officers who took part and includes biographical sketches of most of them." He flipped through the book, found the page he was looking for, and rested a finger on it. "There's General Fargo. You can see that I don't look much like him."

That was true, Gabriel saw as he studied the old, sepia-toned photograph reproduced in the book. Krakowski was rather moon-faced and balding under his campaign cap. General Granville Fordham Fargo had been a lean, intense-looking man with deep-set eyes, a lantern jaw, a mane of salt-and-pepper hair, and a close-cropped beard. Even in the photograph, he had an air of command about him, which wasn't surprising considering that he had led a cavalry regiment.

Gabriel scanned the biographical sketch of Fargo that accompanied the photograph, but nothing unusual jumped out of it. Fargo had been born and raised on a Georgia plantation and had been a planter, surveyor, and college professor before the war. Seemed to have spent his entire life happily within the confines of the state— until the war, at least. He had helped form the Fifth Georgia when the war began and had risen to command it by the time of the battle at Olustee in 1864.

There was nothing in the brief account to explain the events of the past day. Gabriel felt a twinge of frustration.

"Did Fargo contribute one of the accounts of the battle that are in this book?" he asked.

Krakowski shook his head. "No, that wouldn't have been possible."

"Why not? Was he killed in the fighting?" Gabriel glanced at the biographical sketch again and saw that it listed no date of death.

"Oh, no, General Fargo survived the battle and the war itself. But then . . . he disappeared."

Gabriel frowned. "What do you mean?"

"Most people think that the war was completely over once General Lee signed the surrender terms at Appomattox," Krakowski said. "But that's not actually the case. There were Confederate army forces spread out all over the South, and some of them refused to concede defeat. That's what happened with General Fargo and some of his men. Most of the regiment went home once they got word of Lee's surrender, but General Fargo wasn't ready to give up. Instead of going back to Georgia, he and the other holdouts went west instead, across Alabama, Mississippi, and Louisiana. The last anyone knows for sure, they were in Texas, heading south to the Rio Grande."

"They were going to Mexico," Gabriel guessed.

"Probably. A number of Confederate officers believed that if they fled to Mexico or even further, to South America, they could keep the dream of the Confederacy alive down there. General Fargo was one of that group."

Krakowski shrugged. "Most of them eventually gave up and came home, but not General Fargo. He was never heard from again."

If the man had ended up in Mexico or South America, that might at least be a tenuous link between the Fifth Georgia Cavalry and Mariella Montez, Gabriel thought. If she was from that area, her family could have wound up somehow with the general's battle flag and passed it on down through the generations. Fargo might well have had that bottle of Old Pinebark whiskey with him, too, and the empty bottle could have become another family keepsake.

This theory didn't answer a hell of a lot—it didn't explain why she'd thought Michael would be interested in these relics, or why anyone else would be willing to kill over them—but it was a start.

"Would you happen to know anything about the Fifth Georgia's battle flag?" he asked Krakowski.

"Which one?"

"They had more than one?"

Krakowski nodded. "They had two. They had the standard regimental battle flag, the one I'm sure you've seen, the flag known as the Stars and Bars." The man made a face, as if a bad taste had suddenly filled his mouth. "You know, the one that everyone hates because all the skinheads and white supremacist groups like it so much."

"Of course."

"They've got the Fifth Georgia's regimental in a museum in Mexico City. That's one of the reasons people are fairly sure General Fargo made it at least that far. We've been in contact with the museum to see if perhaps they might be willing to return it to us, but so far that arrangement hasn't been worked out."

"Got it," Gabriel said. "And the other flag?"

"That's one I'm pretty sure you haven't seen," Krakowski said, and Gabriel restrained himself from saying, *Don't be so sure*. "That one was General Fargo's personal standard. I've seen a drawing of it made during the war, but the actual flag itself has never been found."

"What did it look like?"

"I wish I could draw it for you," Krakowski said, "it was really quite impressive. But I'm no good at all with a pencil. It had a red background with crossed sabers in the corners, and a circular painting in the middle with a cavalryman on a rearing horse in the foreground. Very striking. It must have been something to see, flying at the front of the regiment as they went into battle. You can hardly imagine."

"I think I can," Gabriel said. "Do you know how the museum in Mexico got hold of the flag they have?"

Krakowski shook his head. "I'm afraid you'd have to ask the director down there. It's not unusual for American artifacts to turn up in Mexico, however. The two countries are side by side, after all, and there's always been a lot of traffic both ways across the border." He paused. "I must say, it's unusual for anyone to be so interested in a figure as obscure as General Fargo. He really doesn't have much historical significance. And to be asked about him twice in the course of one month—"

Gabriel looked up sharply from the book containing the general's portrait and biography. "Twice?" he said.

"That's right. A couple of men were here late last month doing research on him. They claimed to be distant relatives . . . descendants, I mean. But they didn't really look like genealogists."

"Let me guess," Gabriel said. "One of them was a big guy, short blond hair, nose that's been broken a couple of times, scars on his cheeks and around the eyes?"

Krakowski nodded. "That's right. Do you know him?"

"We've met," Gabriel said. "Who was with him?"

"They didn't give me their names," Krakowski said with a shake of his head. "The other man was older. Gray haired and very distinguished looking, with a narrow mustache and these moles, two of them, right over the mustache, on his upper lip. They left a generous cash donation to support our programs."

The description of the second man didn't ring any bells, but he was sure the first man was the same one who had tried twice to kill him in the past twenty-four hours. He said, "They didn't leave you a card, or any way to get in touch with them?"

"I'm afraid not. I just helped them with their research. It's why I have all this information at my fingertips. When they came, they had to wait while I hunted it down, took the better part of an hour just to find this book."

"I'm sure they were glad to wait," Gabriel said. He reached for his wallet. "I appreciate your help myself, Mr. Krakowski."

"Oh, I wasn't hinting for a donation," the man said hastily. "Of course, anything you want to give will be put to good use, but I just enjoy meeting someone else who's interested in the war. Anyway, like I said, we're not officially open today . . . oh, my God."

Gabriel looked up sharply. Krakowski was staring at the door. Gabriel glanced that way, too, and saw Hoyt Johnson standing there.

The shocking thing, though, was the man standing behind Hoyt with a gun pressed to the old-timer's head.

Chapter 6

"You are a stubborn, troublesome bastard, Hunt," the gunman said.

"You're pretty stubborn yourself, to escape that airboat flipping over like that and come back for more," Gabriel replied.

The killer ground the gun barrel against Hoyt's temple, making the swamp rat grimace in pain. "I'd've let go at him with my shotgun, Mr. Hunt, if I'd seen him in time," Hoyt said, "but he snuck up on me."

A stunned Stephen Krakowski regained his voice and stammered, "Th-that's him. One of the men who came here asking about General Fargo!"

"I figured as much," Gabriel said. He asked the gunman, "What do you want?"

"Right now, just for you to leave us alone."

"Let Hoyt go and I give you my word—"

Gabriel didn't get a chance to finish what he was saying. The man pulled the gun barrel away from Hoyt's head, pointed it at Gabriel, and said, "I don't trust your word."

Gabriel flung himself aside as the gun roared. The glass in the display case behind him exploded as the bullet hit it. Krakowski yelled in fear and pain as slivers of glass stung him. The reenactor's rifle was leaning against the case and Gabriel grabbed it as he rolled across the floor. When he surged up onto his feet the gunman fired again, the bullet shattering another case.

Gabriel didn't know if the rifle was loaded or not; probably not. But that was the wonderful thing about these old rifles. They didn't need to be loaded in order to do damage. Gabriel raised the bayonet point and charged.

The guman tried to fire again, but Hoyt picked that moment to make a break for it, twisting and writhing in the gunman's grasp. He wasn't strong enough to break free from his captor's grip, but he forced the man to turn halfway around to hang on to him.

Gabriel struck in grim silence, thrusting the bayonet past Hoyt and into the shoulder of the man's gun arm. The killer howled in pain as his fingers opened involuntarily and the gun hit the floor. He maintained his grip on Hoyt with his other hand, though, and used it to throw the old-timer at Gabriel. The impact made Gabriel stumble backward. While Gabriel struggled to disentangle himself without hurting the old man, the killer ripped the bayonet from his shoulder, threw it aside, and shoved open the glass door behind him. He lunged out into the muggy sunshine with blood welling between the fingers of the hand he was using to clutch his injured shoulder.

Gabriel scrambled after him, scooping up the gun the man had dropped. While he was at it, he pulled the Colt from his waistband. Armed with both pistols, he ran to the door.

The glass shattered as he started to push it open. Gabriel ducked back. It meant the gunman hadn't been alone. He had at least one accomplice outside—maybe the second Jet Skier? Gabriel risked a look and saw the injured man disappearing into the pine forest. Muzzle flashes came from the shadowy gloom under the trees, and Gabriel had to dart for cover as several more bullets stitched through the space where the glass door had been.

"Stay down," he yelled to Hoyt and Krakowski.

"You bet," Hoyt called from behind a display case. When Gabriel glanced around he saw that Krakowski was crouched there, too.

No more shots came from the forest, though, and after a few moments Gabriel decided that the gunman and his accomplice probably had fled. He waited a while longer to be sure.

"Are they gone?" Krakowski asked.

"I think so."

"I'm going to call 911 and get the sheriff's department out here," Krakowski said. "They'll know what to do."

"Hoyt, do you think you can take me back where we came from?" Gabriel was careful not to mention their destination, so Krakowski wouldn't know where they were headed.

"You don't figure I'm gonna argue with a fella holdin' two guns, do you?"

"Wait a minute," Krakowski protested. "You have to wait for the police—"

"Sorry," Gabriel said. "I can't do that." Pocketing the killer's gun, he took two hundred-dollar bills from his pocket and laid them on one of the display cases that hadn't been shattered by flying lead. "That'll pay for some of the damage, and I'll see to it that the rest of it is taken care of later."

"But . . . but . . . those men may still be out there! They could shoot at you again!"

"Not likely. The way he was bleeding, that guy will need medical attention pretty quickly."

"That's one of them," Hoyt said. "The other—"

"It's a chance I'll take." Gabriel looked at Krakowski and said, "Quickly, is there anything else you can tell me about Fargo and the Fifth Georgia? Anything you told them that you didn't tell me?"

"N-no. I can't think of anything. I'm sorry."

"Don't be. You've been a big help. I'm sorry to put you in harm's way."

Gabriel walked outside, Hoyt trailing close behind, broken glass crunching under their feet as they went. Hoyt cast a few nervous glances at the pine forest, but no shots came from the trees as they hurried along the road toward the dock where the airboat was tied up.

Hoyt heaved a sigh of relief when they came in sight of the craft. "I was afraid those sons o' bitches might've sunk her or shot up the motor."

"Better check it over before you crank it," Gabriel suggested. He didn't think his enemies had had time to plant a bomb on the boat, but it never hurt to make sure of these things.

"Oh, yeah, good idea," Hoyt agreed. "Those fellas you're goin' up against won't stop at much, will they?"

"From what I've seen, they won't stop at anything," Gabriel said.

To give Hoyt credit, the old-timer didn't demand to know what it was all about, which was good because Gabriel still didn't know. He just checked over the airboat, reported that nobody had tampered with it, and started the motor. They swung away from the dock and Hoyt pointed the craft back toward St. Augustine.

The roar of the motor was too loud for conversation, which was all right with Gabriel. He used the time to replay in his head everything that had happened and to consider what he had learned from Krakowski.

Instincts honed by years of dealing with trouble told Gabriel that General Granville Fordham Fargo was the key to the whole thing—though how that could be, more than a century after the man lived, he couldn't say. Mariella Montez, whoever she was, had been in possession of a flag that had definitely belonged to the general, as well as an old whiskey bottle that might have. She had come to the reception to give those two items to the Hunt Foundation, prompting a gang of gunmen to try to stop her. Mariella herself had to be important, too, and not only because she'd had the flag and the bottle. Otherwise they wouldn't have kidnapped her.

The last place anyone had seen General Fargo was Texas, Krakowski had said, but Gabriel thought it was safe to assume that the general had made it into Mexico. Otherwise the Fifth Georgia's other battle flag wouldn't have wound up in the museum in Mexico City.

Again, it was only a slender lead . . . but a slender lead was better than none. It was time he made it to Mexico City himself, Gabriel decided.

"We agreed on three hundred bucks," Hoyt protested.

"That was before you got shot at not once but twice," Gabriel said as he pressed five hundred-dollar bills into the old-timer's hand and closed Hoyt's fingers around them. "You earned this, that's for sure."

"Well . . . I ain't gonna argue with you. We'll just say that some of it's for bein' ignorant when the cops ask me about it. I won't know where you came from or where you're goin'. All I know is you waved a gun in my face and made me do what you told me."

Gabriel grinned. "Thanks, Hoyt. If they ever catch up to me, that's what I'll tell them, too."

They were back at the Ponce de Leon Harbor marina

in St. Augustine now, having made it without any more trouble. It was early afternoon, and even though Gabriel hadn't had any lunch yet, he wasn't going to take the time for it. He shook hands with Hoyt, bid the old swamp rat farewell, and headed to the motel to pick up his gear and the rental car.

He kept an eye out for the cops, thinking that Krakowski might have already put them on his trail, but he didn't even sight a police cruiser on his way to the airport.

A short time later he was in the air, talking by radio with Michael and filling him in on everything that had happened in Florida.

"Good Lord! They tried to kill you *twice today*?"

"It just proves that whatever we're dealing with is pretty important," Gabriel said. "To someone, anyway. Of course, we knew that when they tried to kill me twice yesterday. Not to mention when they were willing to shoot up the Metropolitan Museum."

Michael's voice came crackling through the radio's static. "I don't suppose it would do any good to try to talk you out of continuing with this."

"None whatsoever. And you don't really want me to. You don't want the bastards to get away with it, either."

"I suppose not. And there's Miss Montez to consider, too."

"Exactly. We may be the only ones who can help her."

"You mean *you* may be. I'm not doing anything."

"There's plenty for you to do," Gabriel said. "Find out which museum in Mexico City has that other flag and wangle me an introduction to whoever runs the place."

"Consider it done," Michael agreed. "There's not a museum the Foundation doesn't have some connection with."

"There you go," Gabriel said. "Just get the information for me as soon as you can."

Gabriel signed off and concentrated on his flying. He was over the Gulf of Mexico, a seemingly endless expanse of dark blue water. Eventually a green line appeared on the horizon to the south. That was the Yucatan Peninsula, Gabriel knew.

Not long after that a radio call came in from Michael. "I've located the flag," he told Gabriel. "It's at the Museum of the Americas, a small museum affiliated with the university down there. The director is a Dr. Almanzar. I don't know his first name and didn't speak directly with him, but his assistant arranged for you to meet with him this evening at the museum."

Gabriel let out a whistle of admiration. "That's fast work, Michael. Maybe this Dr. Almanzar can tell me how the museum came to get its hands on Fargo's flag in the first place."

"Let's hope so. And that this leads to some actual answers and not just more questions."

He had outraced the sun, so it was only late afternoon when he landed in Mexico City and went through customs. He had worried a little that the Florida authorities, not to mention the ones in New York, might have put out an international alert for him since hell seemed to start popping everywhere he went, but if the Mexican customs officers knew anything about the troubles back in the States, they gave no sign of it. Gabriel passed through without any problems, rented a car, and headed for the hotel where he stayed every time he was in Mexico City.

He took the bag containing the flag and the bottle fragment with him off the plane. He had decided that he wasn't going to let it out of his possession again.

By the time evening was settling down over the vast city in its high mountain basin, Gabriel had showered, shaved, put on fresh clothes, and eaten a decent room service meal washed down with strong Mexican coffee. When he left the hotel he felt considerably refreshed.

Although affiliated with the national university, the Museum of the Americas was located in Chapultepec Park, downtown, rather than on the university campus. The large park was the site of several museums and one of the city's cultural centers, Gabriel recalled from previous visits to the city. A purplish sunset hung in the sky as he parked in front of the small but still impressive stone building.

The main entrance was locked, but a security guard let him in when he called through the glass in fluent Spanish that he had an appointment with Dr. Almanzar and gave his name. The guard consulted a clipboard and then unlocked the door, ushering Gabriel inside. The man pointed down a hallway lined on both sides with display cases and large paintings and said, "Dr. Almanzar's office is at the far end."

"*Gracias,*" Gabriel said. The lighting in the hallway was subdued, but it was enough for him to see various items in the cases as he walked past them. He looked for the battle flag Krakowski had described but didn't see it. The paintings on the walls depicted various scenes from every period of Mexico's history.

Gabriel knocked on the door at the end of the hall, and a woman's voice told him in Spanish to come in. He opened the door and stepped into an office cluttered with books and papers. The woman stood beside the desk, frowning at a book in her hands. This must be the assistant, Gabriel figured. Though she didn't appear very scholarly in a dark blue, form-fitting halter dress that looked like she was ready to go out for an evening on the town.

"Hello," he said. "My name is Gabriel Hunt. I'm supposed to meet with Dr. Almanzar—"

"I know." She closed the book with a snap of pages and set it on the desk. "My assistant told me about your brother's call. I'm Cierra Almanzar."

Well, thought Gabriel.

Chapter 7

"I don't have much time, Señor Hunt," Dr. Cierra Almanzar said. "What can I do for you?"

"I'm here about General Granville Fordham Fargo."

She nodded. "Carlos mentioned as much. We have the battle flag of General Fargo's cavalry regiment here at the museum. It's not on display at the moment, but I can arrange for you to see it."

"That would be helpful, thank you. But what I'm especially interested in is how it came to be here."

"In a Mexican museum, you mean?"

"That's right."

"We have numerous American artifacts and documents in our collection. Any time one of your countrymen came down here to my country to live, he brought at least some of his possessions with him. Over time certain of those items find their way into museums. Quite a number of Confederate military men came to Mexico after the Civil War, I understand, including your General Fargo." Dr. Almanzar ran her eyes up and down Gabriel's rangy form. "You are doing research on the American Civil War?"

"You could say that."

"I mean no offense, Señor Hunt, but you do not strike me as the scholarly type." A smile spread over Gabriel's face. "What?"

"Nothing," Gabriel said. "It's just that I was thinking exactly the same thing about you when I first saw you."

She returned his smile. "I have an event I am expected to attend tonight. I do not normally dress like this." A crease suddenly appeared on her forehead and she snapped her fingers. "Wait a moment. Gabriel Hunt. Of course. You were the one who located the Dumari Temple in Indonesia a couple of years ago!"

Gabriel shrugged.

"Michael Hunt's brother," Dr. Almanzar went on. "Of course." She pushed a lock of raven hair back from her lovely, olive-skinned face. "I read your parents' book. I was sorry to hear about what happened to them."

Gabriel shrugged again, his smile fading. Nine years had passed since their disappearance at sea, eight since they'd been declared dead. With everything he'd managed to find in that time, all the headline-making discoveries, he'd been able to make no headway at all on what had happened to them, and it continued to gnaw at him.

"I'm sorry, Dr. Almanzar, but if you have another engagement, perhaps we'd better get started . . ."

"It's just a fund-raiser for the museum." Her tone of voice made it clear that she considered the event a chore. "I can be a little late if I need to. You wish to see the general's flag?"

"Yes, and I'd like to know as much about its provenance as I can."

She gestured with an elegant hand toward the computer on her desk. "I'll check our records and see what I can find out. While I'm doing that, you can ask Carlos to let you into the Special Collections room. The flag is stored there."

"Carlos is your assistant?"

"That's right." Dr. Almanzar sat down at the keyboard and began clicking away. "I'll join you there in a few minutes."

Gabriel nodded and left the office.

Carlos turned out to be the man he'd thought was a security guard. He led him down another short hallway to a locked door, produced a ring of keys and unlocked it. The large room on the other side of the door was full of shelves and display cases. Gabriel saw pre-Columbian statuary and pottery, stone knives and axes, some sort of feathered headdress, tapestries and paintings, and glass-topped cases full of documents.

When Gabriel asked, Carlos said, "The American Civil War stuff is over there," pointing to the left-hand wall. "Your country is very fortunate, *amigo*."

"Why do you say that?" Gabriel asked.

"You've only had one Civil War. Mexico has had so many we lose track of them."

Carlos left Gabriel in front of the Civil War artifacts, but not before issuing a warning not to touch anything until Dr. Almanzar got there. Gabriel agreed. He leaned over the case where the flag was displayed and studied it through the glass.

As Stephen Krakowski had said, it was a standard Confederate battle flag, two diagonal rows of stars intersecting in the middle of a red field. Tattered around the edges, and with a hole in it that had probably been made by a minié ball. Gabriel didn't see anything unusual about it.

He straightened as he heard the click of high heels in the hallway outside. Dr. Almanzar came in a moment later with a couple of pages she had printed out from the computer in her office.

"This is actually quite interesting," she said. "It seems that the museum acquired the flag from a private collector in Villahermosa in the early twentieth century."

"So it's been here for a hundred years?"

"That's correct."

"Where did the private collector get it?"

"That sort of information would not necessarily be in our records . . . but in this case, it is. The flag was handed down to him from his grandfather, who claimed it was given to him in return for a service by 'the gringo warlord.' "

"The gringo warlord?" Gabriel repeated.

She showed him the section of the printout where that very phrase appeared. "There is apparently a legend in the Chiapas region of a white man from the north who came there to raise an army with the goal of returning to overthrow the invaders who had enslaved his homeland. He disappeared somewhere in the jungle along the border between Mexico and Guatemala and was never seen again."

"General Fargo?"

Dr. Almanzar shrugged. "Perhaps. The warlord's name is long since lost to history, Señor Hunt. But given the history of this flag, it seems at least a likely possibility."

"Chiapas is a pretty rough area," Gabriel mused. "Lots of rebels down there."

Dr. Almanzar made a face. "Lots who call themselves rebels. Politics is often nothing more than an excuse for banditry. I don't know why you are so interested in General Fargo, but if you are thinking of going to Chiapas to look for more information, I would advise against it. You might find yourself in much danger."

"I'm afraid I may not have a choice," Gabriel said.

"No academic pursuit is worth your life." She paused. "But then I forget who I am talking to. You discovered that cult of assassins in Nepal, didn't you? And lived to publish those photographs in *National Geographic*. Perhaps you like risking your life."

Gabriel didn't respond to that comment. Instead he took a shot in the dark and asked, "Do you know a woman named Mariella Montez?"

"Mariella Montez . . . ?" After a moment's thought the doctor shook her head. "No, I'm afraid not. Although there's something familiar about the name . . ." She looked at the printouts again. "That's why, of course. The private collector who sold this flag to the museum, his name was Enrique Montez."

Gabriel felt a familiar thrill go through him, the thrill of knowing that he was on the trail of something important. The leads he'd managed to turn up, slender though they had been, were taking him in the right direction. His instincts had not betrayed him.

Before he could say anything else, though, the sound of a heavy thump, like something falling to the floor, came through the open doorway. Dr. Almanzar heard it, too, and turned in that direction.

"Carlos?" she called. "Are you all right?"

There was no answer.

Gabriel knew he might be overreacting, but he didn't hesitate. Two long strides took him across the room, where he slapped the light switch off. He caught hold of Dr. Almanzar's arm with his other hand as she crossed toward the doorway. Her bare arm was warm and firm in his grip. He said in an urgent whisper, "Wait."

"Señor Hunt! What are you—"

"Let me take a look."

Gabriel pulled her behind him and eased forward into the doorway. A glance down the corridor showed him the front desk and the door beyond it. Carlos was slumped on the floor behind the desk, blood slowly pooling around his head. He was lying with his face toward Gabriel and even from this distance Gabriel could make out the neat hole in his forehead.

Gabriel hadn't heard a shot. That meant whoever had killed Carlos was using a silencer. Not a street thug, then. More professionals.

He stepped back into the Special Collections room, looked around. There were no other doors or windows that he could see. If they got trapped in here, it would be a dead end, in more senses than one.

"What's happened?" Dr. Almanzar asked in a breathless voice, crowding up behind him.

"I'm afraid your assistant has been killed," Gabriel told her. "Someone shot him in the head."

It was a brutal way to break the news, but he wanted Dr. Almanzar to appreciate what they were up against. There were killers loose in the museum, and while Gabriel knew that he was their real target—either that or they were after the second flag—he also knew they wouldn't shrink from gunning down anyone who got in their way.

Dr. Almanzar had blanched at the news of Carlos's murder. "What are we going to do?"

"There's no other way out of this room?"

Mutely, she shook her head.

"Do you have any sort of security system here?"

"Not really," Dr. Almanzar said. "The collections all have historical value, of course, but none of them are worth enough to tempt thieves. At least, not that we knew of."

"So if I broke some of these display cases, it wouldn't set off an alarm?"

"No. Only the front door. If someone broke the glass there, then an alarm would sound and the police would be alerted."

A grim smile tugged at Gabriel's mouth. "Good enough," he said.

He knew they didn't have much time. The men who had killed Carlos might be coming down the hallway even now. He was carrying the Colt in a shoulder holster tonight and reached under his coat to draw it. He didn't want to get involved in another shootout if he could avoid it, not with Dr. Almanzar there, but it wasn't always possible to avoid such things. Switching the gun to his left hand, he lifted a stone axe from a pair of hooks on the wall with his right.

"What are you doing?" the doctor said. "You can't—"

"Get behind something solid," Gabriel said.

He saw Dr. Almanzar gape at him for a second, then abruptly decide to follow his advice. She scrambled behind a big open cabinet full of what looked like maps.

Gabriel hefted the axe in his hand, judging its weight and balance. He could put a round from the Colt through the museum's front door, but a bullet hole might not be enough to trigger the alarm. And anyway, he didn't know how many adversaries he was facing—he might need all the bullets he had just to deal with them.

He took a deep breath and then stepped through the doorway, raising the axe behind his head as he did so. His arm flashed forward and sent the axe spinning through the air, over the desk, and into the glass of the door. The glass shattered, splintering outward, and instantly an alarm began to blare.

As he'd thrown the axe, Gabriel had seen three figures

clad in black creeping along the walls of the corridor toward the room he was in. Even before his arm descended and the alarm went off, the silenced pistols the men held came up and began to spit death at him. He leaped back through the doorway, narrowly missed by a couple of shots as he did so. The sounds of ricochets echoed from the walls of the corridor.

As he landed, he rolled behind a display case and came to a stop on his stomach. Thrusting the Colt's barrel around the end of the case, he fired as one of the assassins tried to rush into the room. The man cried out as the bullet drove him backward. One of his companions grabbed him and dragged him out of the doorway.

Now the fact that there was only one way in or out of this room played in Gabriel's favor. If the other two men rushed him, he would be able to cut them down as they came through the door. They had to know that as well, and they would be worrying about the alarm, too. They had no way of knowing how soon the police might arrive.

A hand holding a gun poked around the doorjamb. The gun erupted several times as the man emptied it, but he was just flinging lead blindly around the room. The shots shattered some displays but didn't come close to him or Dr. Almanzar.

Then the hand vanished and he heard the swift rataplan of running footsteps as the men fled.

Dr. Almanzar heard it, too. "Are . . . are they gone?" she asked.

"Stay where you are," Gabriel said. "It could be a trick."

He didn't want to wait too long, though, because *he* didn't want to have to deal with the police, either. Any bureaucracy was bad enough; the Mexican legal system was worse than most. He could easily wind up being held in jail for days, maybe even longer.

After a couple of minutes he got up and risked a look in the hallway. It was deserted. Gabriel held out a hand to Dr. Almanzar and said, "Come on."

She emerged from behind the cabinet, hesitated a second, then took his hand. "Where are we going?"

"That's up to you, as long as it's away from here."

"But the police—"

"—will be very upset that we left before they got here, I know. But I'll live with the guilt." He held one elbow out to her. "You say you're expected at an event?"

Chapter 8

For a moment Gabriel thought that Dr. Almanzar was going to argue with him, maybe even fight to get away.

Then she said, "This interest in General Fargo's flag is not just a matter of academic research, is it?"

Gabriel shook his head. "No."

"Then perhaps we should take it with us," she said as she slipped her hand out of his, went to the display case, and unlocked it with a small key she took from a pocket in her dress.

Gabriel grinned as Dr. Almanzar took the flag from the case and folded it carefully. "I can put it under my jacket," he suggested.

"Can I return to my office for my bag?" she asked as he stowed away the flag, nestling it next to the other flag, which he'd tucked into the waistband of his pants at the small of his back before heading to the museum. Good thing they made flags of thin fabric back then, he thought. It was getting a bit tight as it was.

"Okay," he said. "But make it quick." The alarm was still going off and it was only a matter of time before someone showed up.

They hurried out of the Special Collections room,

Gabriel going first just in case one of the black-clad assassins had remained behind and was waiting in ambush for them. No shots came their way, though, as they headed toward Dr. Almanzar's office.

"There's a back door we can use," she said once she had collected her purse.

"Excellent," Gabriel said. He'd noticed how the doctor avoided looking at Carlos's corpse as they passed the security station, but other than that she seemed to be holding up well, considering.

She led the way to a rear door and pushed it open. It was very dark back here in the shadow of the trees of Chapultepec Park, but Dr. Almanzar seemed to know her way around. A couple of vehicles were parked in the small lot she led him to, and she headed straight for one of them, a jeep with enclosed sides.

"Looks like something you'd use for field work," Gabriel commented as Dr. Almanzar unlocked the jeep's doors.

"It is. Get in."

"You're driving?"

She patted the jeep's hood and smiled. "This is my *niño*. No offense, Señor Hunt, but if there's a chance anyone is going to be coming after us, I'd rather be at the wheel."

Gabriel nodded and swung into the passenger seat. "Let's go." If this turned out to be an attempt to double-cross him, he would deal with that problem then.

Dr. Almanzar knew all the roads through the park and sent the jeep twisting and turning along them, emerging a few minutes later at Paseo de la Reforma, the wide, busy boulevard that cut through the northern section of the park. As the doctor turned west on the boulevard,

Gabriel heard whooping sirens and looked back to see flashing red and blue lights through the trees.

The police had arrived at the museum. They would find the shattered door, Carlos's body, and the damage in the Special Collections room.

What they wouldn't find was the man Gabriel had shot. Once again, the killers had taken their fallen comrade with them. That might almost have been an honorable gesture—if Gabriel hadn't suspected that it was motivated purely by self-interest. The bastards were savvy enough to know better than to leave any evidence behind that might lead the authorities to them.

Dr. Almanzar navigated through the heavy traffic on the boulevard like someone who was accustomed to it. As she drove, she said in a brisk voice, "Considering that you almost got me killed tonight, Señor Hunt, don't you think you should tell me what this is all about?"

Gabriel hesitated. He didn't want to draw her any deeper into this affair than she already was.

"You have an event to attend," he said. "If you'll drop me back at my hotel, you can go on to that and forget about everything that's happened tonight."

"Until the police arrive to question me, you mean."

"Well, there's that to consider," Gabriel admitted. "You can always claim that you met with me, saw me out, and then left yourself, and that everything was fine when you did. The break-in and Carlos's murder could have happened after you were gone."

"I suppose, but I won't have an alibi. And neither will you. Did you rent a car?"

"I did," Gabriel said. "But I paid cash for it and used a phony driver's license. The police won't be able to trace it back to me."

She glanced over at him. "Do you always cover your trail like a criminal, Señor Hunt?"

"Often. A lot of times in my work it's better if I don't get any meddling from the local authorities."

"So you believe it's all right to flout the laws of another country, eh?"

"Oh, I flout the laws of the United States, too," Gabriel said. "When I have to."

She glanced at him again and then, after a moment, laughed. "You're *un hombre loco*, aren't you, Señor Hunt?"

Gabriel sensed the tension between them easing. "Why don't you call me Gabriel?"

She said, "All right, Gabriel. Then I'm Cierra. I guess once you've been shot at together, there's no more point in formality."

"My thinking exactly," Gabriel said.

"I still want to know what this is about. Why don't you tell me on the way to the event?"

"You're still going? And you're taking me?"

"I'm sure the host would like to meet you," she said.

"As long as he's not the chief of police," Gabriel said.

Gabriel wasn't sure this was the best idea, but he supposed a magnificent villa in the exclusive Lomas de Chapultepec residential district west of the city was as good a place as any to wait and see if the police were going to connect him with what had happened at the museum.

"The estate belongs to Vladimir Antonio de la Esparza," Cierra Almanzar explained. "He's one of the museum's largest benefactors. He's thinking about making another very generous donation. That is why I couldn't say no when he asked me to come to this party tonight. I hope he's not offended that I'll be showing up an hour late."

"You could always tell him you were delayed by three assassins," Gabriel suggested.

She shot him an angry look. "I cannot take this as lightly as you, Señor Hunt. Carlos was my friend, and he leaves a wife and four children."

"I'm sorry," Gabriel said without hesitation.

She nodded.

"In this traffic, it should take us at least half an hour to reach Señor Esparza's villa," Cierra said, her tone thawing. "Is that enough time for you to tell me why those men wanted you dead, and what your interest is in General Fargo's battle flag?"

"I think so," Gabriel said. He launched into the tale, thinking as he did so about how many events, how much danger, had been packed into the past twenty-four hours. It had been a hurricane, and he was lucky to have survived it. And the storm wasn't over yet.

He had to give Cierra credit. She didn't interrupt as he laid out the facts for her. When he finished, she drove silently for a full minute before saying, "You expect me to believe this?"

"Every word of it is true," Gabriel insisted. "You have my word on that."

"The word of a man who has admitted breaking laws, who has counseled me to lie—"

"Only for the best reasons."

Cierra fell silent again, obviously trying to digest everything he had told her. After a few moments, during which she continued to weave in and out of traffic, she said, "It is an incredible story, Gabriel. But incredible things happen sometimes. You have no idea what's behind these attempts on your life?"

He shook his head. "Just that it must involve General Fargo's legacy somehow. Maybe when he went to Mexico, he took part of the Confederate treasury with him?"

"If he did, it was stolen from him within days. Even then, Chiapas was full of bandits." Cierra turned from the boulevard onto a smaller road that led up into hills topped with expensive villas. Gabriel could see the lights of those estates, hanging over the city like stars. "This Mariella Montez . . . you say she is very beautiful?"

Was that a tone of jealousy he heard in her voice, Gabriel wondered? If so, it came as something of a surprise.

"She was . . . striking," he said.

"You mean beautiful."

"Well . . . yes." Facts were facts.

"She must be a descendant of Enrique Montez, the man who sold the flag to the museum a hundred years ago," Cierra mused. "The family must have had both flags and hung on to the other one for some reason."

Gabriel nodded. "That's the way I see it, too." An idea occurred to him. "Maybe she wanted me to go to Chiapas and find the general's trail."

"After a century and a half?"

"I've found older things than that."

"True enough," Cierra said. "But you said she was not seeking you, she was seeking your brother. What century-old trails has he ever followed?"

For that, Gabriel didn't have an answer.

"I'll tell you again, Gabriel, it would not be a good idea for you to go to Chiapas. It's dangerous enough for the people who live there, let alone outsiders."

Something in her voice intrigued him. "You sound like you know quite a bit about the area."

"I ought to. I was born and raised there."

That surprised him, too. From looking at her, he'd have said Cierra had more Castilian blood than Indian, and he knew that Indians dominated the population of the Chiapas region.

She must have sensed his reaction, because she explained, "My father was the manager of a coffee plantation." Her voice hardened as she went on, "He and my mother were killed by bandits while I was studying at the university. I've never gone back. It wouldn't have done me any good if I did. The bandits took over the plantation."

"I'm sorry," Gabriel said.

"So you see, I know what it's like to lose one's parents. Perhaps that is why I'm willing to help you if I can, Gabriel. We have a . . . kinship."

They had more than that, Gabriel thought as he sensed the attraction between them growing.

The road they had been following wound around a steep hillside and finally emerged at the top of the slope, where a huge, sprawling, brightly lit Spanish-style villa sat in the midst of well-manicured lawns and gardens. A number of expensive cars were already parked there, and Cierra's jeep looked a bit out of place as she slid it in among them.

"You had better leave your gun in the jeep," Cierra said as they got out.

"I don't care much for that idea."

"Señor Esparza is a very rich man. Because of that he and his family are likely targets for kidnapping. He has many bodyguards, and you won't be allowed in the house if you're armed."

What she said made sense. Gabriel didn't like it, but he removed his jacket, stripped off the shoulder rig, and placed it and the Colt under the jeep's seat. Cierra locked up the vehicle.

Lanterns burned in the limbs of the trees that overhung the driveway. The sweet, heavy fragrance of flowers filled the air. Along with the floral scent, the place reeked of money.

His dark suit wasn't quite good enough for a cocktail party in luxurious surroundings like this, Gabriel thought, but it would do. Particularly with Cierra on his arm. No one would be looking at him.

After a couple of tough-looking bodyguards waved metal detector wands over him, as Cierra had warned would happen, a poker-faced butler who wouldn't have been out of place in a British manor let them in the door and escorted them into the ballroom where the party was taking place. It was crowded with exactly the sort of beautiful, brittle people he'd seen a day earlier at the Met in New York. Only with better tans. Gabriel could never understand how Michael could bear to spend his days in circles like these. Gabriel could move among them easily enough . . . but he didn't like them.

"There's Señor Esparza," Cierra said. She nodded toward a man making his way through the crowd toward them. Like Moses at the Red Sea, the mass of people parted before him, indicating that no matter how much wealth was in this room tonight, this man was the richest, or the most powerful, or very likely both.

He was also, Gabriel thought as he noted the man's gray hair and distinguished appearance and the two moles above his narrow mustache, the man Stephen Krakowski had described that morning at the Olustee battlefield—the one who had accompanied the broken-nosed killer on a quest for information about General Granville Fordham Fargo.

Chapter 9

"Cierra!" Señor Vladimir Antonio de la Esparza said with a big smile of welcome. "I was afraid you weren't going to be able to make it!"

"I was delayed," she said as he put his hands on her bare shoulders and leaned forward to kiss her cheek.

"No trouble, I hope."

"No, just business." That was an outright lie, of course, and Esparza would realize it if the police showed up looking to question her about Carlos's murder. Gabriel hoped it would take them a while to get around to that.

Of course, Esparza might already know it was a lie—if he was the one who'd sent the assassins to the museum in the first place.

Cierra turned and held out a hand toward Gabriel. "I hope it's all right that I brought along a colleague of mine. This is Señor Gabriel Hunt."

Esparza's rather bushy gray eyebrows rose. "Of the Hunt Foundation?"

"You may be thinking of my brother, Michael, Señor Esparza," Gabriel said coolly. "I don't really get involved."

"You are too modest," Esparza said. "My business is communications, but my passion is history and archeology. I've been fortunate enough to help numerous museums acquire items for their collections, including our dear Cierra's, of course, and naturally in the course of those efforts I've heard of both the Hunt Foundation and the illustrious Gabriel Hunt."

He put out a hand. Gabriel shook it. "Illustrious," Gabriel said. "That's a new one for me. More often I hear 'notorious.'"

"Well . . . one has to be a bit of a pirate to be a successful explorer, eh?" Esparza grinned. "Welcome to my villa, Señor Hunt. Please, make yourself at home."

"*Gracias,* Señor Esparza."

Waiters were moving around the room, carrying trays of drinks. Gabriel's jaw tightened as Esparza motioned one of the men over. This reminded him too much of what had happened at the Metropolitan Museum the night before. These waiters wore white jackets instead of red, but still, their presence made him tense.

He reminded himself that waiters carried drinks around cocktail parties all the time. It didn't have to mean anything.

He accepted a margarita from one waiter and sipped it while Cierra made small talk with Esparza. From her appearance and manner you'd never have guessed that she'd gone through a shootout and a friend's murder less than an hour earlier. He supposed that Cierra's upbringing in a dangerous area like Chiapas had given her steadier nerves than most people.

Esparza turned to Gabriel and asked, "Are you going to be doing business with the museum, Señor Hunt? Selling some artifact you've acquired, perhaps?"

"As a matter of fact, I've recently put my hands on a

nice item Dr. Almanzar might be interested in," Gabriel replied. "Just last night, in fact."

Was that a flicker of something more than polite interest in Esparza's eyes, Gabriel asked himself, or just his imagination?

For a man who didn't believe in coincidences, he thought, he was asking himself to accept a rather large one: that Cierra would bring him right to the home of the man who was behind the bloody attack at the Met and the ensuing attempts on Gabriel's own life.

And yet perhaps it wasn't a coincidence at all. The whole affair was tied in with those flags of General Fargo's, and the flags' trail led right to the Museum of the Americas. Esparza's connection with the museum could have put him onto something that had prompted the violence. Esparza could have found out somehow that Mariella was taking the general's personal standard to New York and been willing to go to any lengths to stop her from turning it over to the Hunt Foundation.

The hidden flags seemed to burn against Gabriel's back as that thought went through his head. To incite the ruthless brutality Gabriel had seen since last night, the flags had to be very valuable indeed.

He wondered what Esparza would do if he knew that Gabriel had the flags on him at this very moment.

He didn't intend for the man to find out. It would be better, Gabriel told himself, if he and Cierra got out of here as soon as they reasonably could.

"You and Cierra are in negotiations concerning this item, then?" Esparza asked, his smile never wavering.

"You could say that. My apologies for keeping her away from your little get-together until now, señor."

Esparza waved a hand. "*De nada*. She is here now, blessing us with her loveliness, and this is all that matters."

He reached over, slid that same hand up Cierra's bare arm, leaned closer to her. "Is this not so, *querida*?"

Her smile shrank a little, Gabriel thought. He wondered how far she'd had to go in the past to secure Esparza's help for the museum . . . not that it was any of his business.

"You're too kind, Vladimir," she murmured.

"Not at all, not at all. Your beauty outshines that of any woman here . . . and your intelligence is far above theirs as well." He looked at Gabriel. "I've always believed that intelligent women are the most attractive, Señor Hunt. What about you?"

"I can't argue with that," Gabriel said. "Unfortunately, Dr. Almanzar and I have to continue our business, so we'll be leaving—"

"So soon?" Gabriel might have been mistaken, but he thought that Esparza's grip tightened on Cierra's arm. She kept her face carefully impassive, though. "That is a great pity. Are you certain it cannot wait until tomorrow?"

"I'm sure," Gabriel said. His nerves had been crawling ever since he entered this luxurious villa, and by now his instincts were yelling for him to get out.

"Well, one cannot stand in the way of history, can one?" Esparza leaned in and kissed Cierra again on the cheek, then shook hands with Gabriel. "Farewell, Señor Hunt. I hope to see you again soon."

"I'm sure we'll run into each other," Gabriel said. He took hold of Cierra's other arm, and for a second she was caught between them, as if they were about to have a tug of war over her.

But then Esparza let go of her, and Gabriel steered her toward the door.

"What was that all about?" Cierra whispered to him as they weaved their way through the crowd.

"Esparza had something to do with what happened at the museum," Gabriel said, keeping his voice low.

Cierra stopped short. "*What?* Are you really *loco*, Gabriel? Vladimir is the museum's biggest benefactor."

"Then he probably knows all about General Fargo's flag and the legend of the gringo warlord, doesn't he?"

Frowning angrily, Cierra stared at him for a moment, but then Gabriel saw doubt begin to creep into her eyes. She was smart enough to know that what he was saying made sense. Or at least that he had no reason to lie about it.

"And he fits the description of the other man who went to Florida to try to find out more about the general," Gabriel went on. "Do you know any of his associates who look like the man I bayoneted?"

"Of course not! The very idea is insane." She paused. "Of course, I don't know everyone who works for Vladimir . . ."

"I didn't think so."

"But that doesn't mean—" She stopped and looked back the way they had come. Gabriel did, too, and they saw Esparza standing on the other side of the room watching them. His affable smile had disappeared, and now he had the look of a predator about him, an intense stare that had locked in on his prey.

"*Dios mio,*" Cierra breathed. "You could be right. He's always been very generous when it comes to the museum, but he has a reputation for ruthlessness in his business."

"And in getting anything else he wants, I'd bet," Gabriel said. "Let's get out of here."

She clutched at his arm. "If he is who you say . . . will he allow us to leave?"

"I think he will. He won't want any trouble in his own home, with all his fancy friends around."

Gabriel was aware of Esparza's hawklike gaze following them all the way out of the ballroom. As they passed the bodyguards, he had to wonder if either of them had been among the groups he'd traded shots with several times recently. It was certainly possible.

Danger seemed to lurk in the shadows along the driveway, but Gabriel and Cierra reached the jeep safely. "Hold on a minute," he said as she reached for the door handle.

He knelt to take a quick look under the vehicle. When he saw nothing unusual there, he lifted the hood and checked under it, too.

"You thought he might try to blow us up?" Cierra asked in an astonished tone.

"Not really. Again, there would be too many awkward questions for him to have to answer, even for a man of his wealth and power. But it never hurts to make sure."

As they climbed into the jeep, Cierra asked, "Where are we going now?"

"Take me back to the hotel and drop me off there. Your part in this is over. Esparza won't bother you. He may suspect that I told you some things I shouldn't have, but he can't know for sure. And he probably thinks he can continue to make use of you in the future, so he won't get rough with you."

Her voice was chilly as she said, "No one uses me, Señor Hunt."

"I just meant that he needs you to remain at the museum."

Cierra started the jeep and backed up, then turned around and drove out through the massive gates at the entrance to the estate. She started down the winding road toward the bottom of the hill.

Gabriel heard the high-pitched growl of motorcycle

engines behind them even before they were out of sight of Esparza's villa.

"Son of a bitch," he said as he reached under the seat for his gun. "I was wrong."

"The notorious Gabriel Hunt, wrong?" Cierra said. "About what?"

"Looks like Esparza wants me dead bad enough that he doesn't care if you have to die, too."

Chapter 10

Cierra stared at him for a second before Gabriel said, "Punch it!" Her foot came down hard on the gas and sent the jeep spurting ahead. She hauled hard on the wheel as the vehicle skidded around a bend in the road.

Gabriel had the Colt in his hand now. He twisted around in the seat to look through the rear window. Four headlights came into view behind them, bobbing and weaving a little as the speeding motorcyclists fought to keep their bikes on the road.

"Déjà vu all over again," Gabriel muttered. Instead of being pursued across the Queensboro Bridge by an SUV full of killers, now he had four assassins on Harleys chasing him down a Mexican hillside.

The big difference was that he wasn't alone tonight.

Cierra Almanzar was with him, and her life was in danger, too.

"Take the turns as fast as you can without sending us off the road," he told her as he started to clamber over the seat into the storage area in the rear of the jeep.

"What are you going to do?"

"Try to even up the odds." He unfastened the flexible rear window and flung it up out of the way.

"Gabriel!"

She sounded alarmed, like something bad had just popped up in front of them. He jerked around to face front again. "What is it?"

"You can't just start shooting at them! They may be innocent—"

The bullet that suddenly shattered the right-hand side mirror ended that argument. Cierra screamed and jerked the wheel involuntarily, sending the jeep in a screeching skid toward the edge of the road.

The drop-off wasn't that far, but it was steep and Gabriel knew that if they went off the road at this speed, chances were neither of them would survive the crash. He was about to lunge back over the seat to grab the wheel and try to right the jeep, but before he could do that, Cierra tightened her grip on the wheel and pulled the vehicle back to the center of the road.

"Sorry," she said. "I'm still not used to being shot at."

"You just keep us on the road," Gabriel said as he turned back to their pursuers. "I'll see what I can do to get them to stop shooting."

He saw muzzle flashes from the bikers, who had closed the gap to about fifty yards. They were able to take the turns faster than Cierra could in the jeep. The bikes leaned far over as their riders careened around the bends in the road.

Luckily, they hadn't run into any other traffic so far on the descent from Esparza's villa. Gabriel hoped it stayed that way. He stuck the Peacemaker out the back of the jeep and squeezed off three shots as he moved the barrel from right to left. Accuracy was next to impossible under these conditions, but the way the motorcyclists were spread out across the road, he thought he had at least a chance of hitting one of them.

One of the bikes suddenly spun out of control. Gabriel didn't know if he'd hit it or its rider or if the gunman had just lost control of the motorcycle. Either way, the rider slammed into the ground and then the bike landed on him with crushing force before bouncing and skidding along the road, sending up sparks. The rider didn't get up.

Then the jeep was around another turn and all of the killers were out of sight for the moment. Gabriel looked around the back of the jeep to see if there was anything else he could use as a weapon.

He spotted a plastic gas can, picked it up and shook it. He heard a sloshing sound. Not full, but maybe half. That would do. He set the can down on the floorboard, pulled the tails of his shirt out of his trousers, and ripped off a thick strip.

"What are you doing back there?" Cierra called over her shoulder.

"Getting ready to set off some fireworks," Gabriel told her. He stuffed the piece of shirt down into the gas can's spout, then tilted the can so that the gas would soak the end of it and seep up the makeshift fuse. When he could smell the sharp tang of it, he knew it was ready.

He had a vintage Zippo lighter in his jacket pocket. He didn't smoke, but he'd found it handy to carry a lighter anyway. There was always a chance you might come across a beautiful woman who needed a light—or a Molotov cocktail. And because they were designed to withstand the rigors of combat, Zippos were extremely reliable. He fished his out now, flipped open the top, and spun the wheel as he held it to the gas-soaked piece of shirt.

The flame caught instantly, flaring up. Cierra glanced over her shoulder and cried out in alarm.

Gabriel was already tossing the gas can out the back of the jeep, though. He heaved it hard, knowing that it would explode in seconds and wanting to be as far away when it did as possible. The can hit the road, bounced once as the motorcyclists saw it and tried to steer around it.

Then a ball of fire bloomed in the night like a red and orange and blue flower, covering the road almost from one side to the other. Gabriel caught a glimpse of two of the bikes being engulfed in it, and then he couldn't see them anymore.

The fourth and final man zoomed his bike toward the hillside, though, driving up on the slope to avoid the burst of flame. Gabriel grimaced as he watched the man wrestle the motorcycle back onto the road, past the fire. The pitch of the bike's engine rose even more as its rider accelerated in pursuit of the jeep.

A horn blared from the other direction, and Cierra said, "Gabriel!"

He twisted around, saw some sort of big, heavy luxury car coming up the hill straight at them. During the last turn, Cierra had been forced to drift out of her lane and into the facing one. They were seconds away from a head-on collision, with a vicious killer coming up behind them.

"Brake!" Gabriel shouted. "Stand on it!"

Cierra slammed both feet on the brake pedal. Rubber screamed against the pavement. Smoke rose from the tires as they locked and skidded. The other vehicle was trying to stop, too.

But the motorcycle was going too fast. Gabriel saw it coming and ducked. At the last second the rider tried to lay the bike down, but he was too late. It slammed into the back of the jeep but the rider kept going, soaring into the air and flying completely over Cierra's *niño*, screaming every bit of the way.

That scream was cut off as the man crunched into the front grille of the luxury car. The car was still moving, and the impact must have pulped every bone in the assassin's body. The car finally rocked to a stop, but not before running over the man as well.

"Go around them," Gabriel told Cierra. She sat hunched over the wheel, breathing heavily.

"What? But shouldn't we check on those people in the car?"

"More of Esparza's men may be on their way. Go around them." He stuck his head out the back window and checked the damage the motorcycle had done when it rear-ended the jeep. The fender was bashed in, but that appeared to be the extent of it.

"Go!" he said again to Cierra, and this time she complied. The jeep was still running. She gave it gas, veered around the stopped car, and shot down the hillside.

A minute later they reached the bottom of the slope. Paseo de la Reforma was nearby, and once they got onto the boulevard, they could blend into the heavy traffic that hardly ever let up, night or day.

"We need a place where Esparza can't find us," Gabriel said.

"Us?" Cierra repeated.

"I didn't want you in the middle of this, but you are. Now that Esparza's seen you with me, he's written you off. Clearly he told those bikers to kill us both."

"Then we should go to the police. We can tell them what happened . . ." Cierra's voice trailed off, and after a moment she said in a dull tone, "That won't work, will it? As much money as Vladimir has, the authorities would never believe us. Even if they did, they wouldn't go against him."

Gabriel nodded. "That's right. I'd say our only chance is to get out of Mexico City and beat Esparza to whatever it is he's after."

"You mean . . ."

"I'm sorry, Cierra."

"We're going to Chiapas, aren't we?"

"And wherever the trail leads us from there."

"Chiapas," he heard her mutter as her hands tightly gripped the wheel. "You know how to make a girl's night, Gabriel Hunt."

Going back to the hotel would be too risky, Gabriel decided, and returning to the museum was out of the question. The police would still be there, and Esparza might have men watching both places. Cierra's apartment wasn't safe either, since Esparza knew where she lived.

"He's never been there, though," she snapped. "So get whatever you were thinking out of your head."

"I wasn't thinking anything," Gabriel lied. "Is there somewhere else we can go that he wouldn't know about?"

Cierra thought it over for a moment, then said, "The old man who was the foreman on the plantation when I was a little girl lives here in Mexico City now. I've tried to keep in touch with him. He's really the closest thing to family I have left from that time. I'm sure I've never mentioned him to Vladimir. And he retired from the plantation so long ago, even if Vladimir investigated my background he wouldn't have turned up Pancho's name."

Gabriel nodded. "He sounds perfect. That is, if you don't mind involving him in this."

"I don't know where else to go." She laughed softly. "And Pancho is a fierce old buzzard. He would feel insulted if he ever found out that I was in trouble and didn't come to him."

"All right. Let's go there now, before Esparza has a chance to pick up our trail again."

A few minutes later Cierra left Paseo de la Reforma and turned onto a highway that led out of the city. "Pancho lives in a *colonia* on the southern edge of town," she explained.

"Does he live alone?" Gabriel asked.

Cierra laughed. "Oh, no. His wife and their children and their grandchildren and great-grandchildren live with him. It's a very extended family."

Gabriel hated to get that many more innocent people involved. "It would probably be a good idea to tell this old friend of yours as little as possible about what's going on," he suggested.

"I'd trust Pancho with my life," she said.

"That's exactly what you'll be doing . . . but I was thinking more for his sake than ours. If he can just give us a place to stay for the night, in the morning we can leave for Chiapas."

Cierra nodded. She was still taking things awfully well, Gabriel thought, considering that just a few hours ago she hadn't thought that the night held anything more than another boring cocktail party among the rich and beautiful at Esparza's villa. The possibility of being surrounded by violence and death had surely never entered her head. Normal people just didn't think about such things.

Which just went to show you, Gabriel thought wryly, how far from normal his life was . . .

It took quite a while in the heavy traffic to reach the *colonia* where Pancho Guzman lived with his large family. It was a lower-middle-class neighborhood with narrow, winding streets but what appeared to be fairly spacious, well-kept houses behind narrow lawns. Cierra brought the jeep to a stop behind a rusty old pickup, in front of a house where one light still burned in a front window. Most of the houses along the street were already dark, because this was a working neighborhood where people turned in early so they could get up and go to their jobs the next morning.

When Gabriel and Cierra got out, Cierra went to the back of the jeep and examined the damage the motorcycle had done when it crashed into the vehicle. With a look of dismay, she shook her head.

"This jeep has been on digs all over the country, in all sorts of wilderness, and never got a scratch on it. Look what happens to it in the fanciest part of Mexico City!" She glared at him for a second and then said, "Come on."

The man who answered her knock stood tall, straight, and broad-shouldered and didn't appear old at first glance. Then Gabriel saw how his face had been darkened to the color of old saddle leather by years of exposure to sun and wind and how hundreds of tiny wrinkles had seamed and gullied his skin. The man's voice boomed out, though, as he said in Spanish, "Cierra! Little one! How are you?"

He threw his arms around her and gave her such an energetic hug that her feet came up off the porch for a second. She laughed as she returned the hug.

"I'm fine, Pancho, but . . . I need help."

The old man let go of her and turned toward Gabriel, his hands clenching into big, knobby-knuckled fists. "Is this gringo bothering you?" he asked in an ominous voice.

"No! No, not at all. This man is a friend. Gabriel Hunt, meet Pancho Guzman."

Gabriel realized now that Pancho had only one eye; the right socket was empty and sunk deep in the weathered face. But the man's left eye glittered with life and intelligence. He stuck out a big right hand and shook with Gabriel.

"Señor Hunt, welcome to my home," Pancho said, switching to English. He looked at Cierra and quirked an eyebrow. "You and this hombre . . . ?"

"We just met tonight, Pancho," she said. "It's not like that. We're . . . business associates, I suppose you could say."

Pancho nodded. "Ah."

"And we need help."

"You said that, little one. Tell me, what can Pancho do?"

"We need a place to stay for the night. Some bad men are after us."

"Bandits?" Pancho growled. "Like in Chiapas?"

"You could almost say that," Gabriel said. "But the less you know about it, the better for you and your family, Señor Guzman. Cierra and I are leaving on an expedition tomorrow, but first we need some sleep and some supplies, and a place to get the doctor's jeep off the street and out of sight, just in case anyone comes looking for it."

Pancho nodded. "I can provide all these things, and I ask for no explanations. The word of this *niña* is good enough for me."

"Thank you, Pancho," Cierra said as she laid a hand on the old man's arm. "I knew I could count on you."

"Always," Pancho vowed. "Your father was a good man, and your mother was a saint. I should have been there to protect them from the evil that came to the plantation."

"Then you would have died, too," Cierra pointed out.

"Yes, but it would have been a good death, fighting those *bastardos*!"

Gabriel hoped that Pancho wouldn't get a chance to die fighting the bastards who were stalking him and Cierra now.

Chapter 11

The next morning, the pickup rattled and bounced along the expressway leading southeast from Mexico City to Puebla. The road was fairly good, but the pickup's suspension was in bad shape. Pancho had told them that he'd intended to get it repaired; he just hadn't gotten around to it yet.

"But the engine, she runs perfect," the old man had claimed, and so far, it seemed to be true. Gabriel felt plenty of power under the dented hood when he pressed down on the gas. The pickup might not be much to look at, but it would get them where they were going.

Gabriel wished he knew exactly where that was.

Trading vehicles with Pancho Guzman had been his idea. Cierra hadn't liked it, but she had to admit it might be safer to take Pancho's pickup and leave her jeep stashed safely out of sight in the shed behind the old foreman's house. Esparza might have men watching all the roads leading out of Mexico City, especially the ones on the southeastern side of the city.

Gabriel was at the wheel, a battered straw Stetson belonging to one of Pancho's sons on his head. He hadn't shaved, and he wore one of Pancho's faded work shirts.

Cierra sat beside him, her hair pulled back in a tight bun behind her head. Gabriel thought she looked good in a white, off-the-shoulder blouse and a long skirt. Their appearance was different enough from the night before that he hoped they would escape notice if Esparza did have men watching the highway.

The pickup's bed was filled with supplies that Pancho's wife had brought back from the market this morning. A tied-down tarp covered the boxes and bags. Pancho had also insisted that they take a lever-action Winchester and a double-barreled shotgun that belonged to him, and his wife had packed ammunition for the weapons, too.

"I don't know what sort of trouble is chasing you, and I don't want to know," the old man had said. "But if it catches up to you, you might need those guns."

Gabriel couldn't argue with that.

They had left before sunrise. To all appearances, they were a young couple, a farmer and his wife, who had come to Mexico City and were now on their way home. If that masquerade was successful, they would be well out of the city before Esparza ever found out that they were gone. With any luck, he might not find out at all.

Gabriel didn't think they would be that lucky. Even if they slipped through the cordon that Esparza was bound to have thrown around the city, the man knew more about what was going on than they did. He had to figure that they would head for Chiapas to pick up the trail of General Fargo. He had gone to a lot of trouble to try to stop Gabriel from interfering with his plans, whatever they were, and he wouldn't stop now.

But maybe they could gain a few days' advantage. Gabriel hoped to, anyway.

Cierra told him where to turn and which roads to

take. He knew Mexico fairly well, but she was the native here, not him, so he trusted her directions.

"It's eight hundred kilometers to the old plantation," she told him as they left Mexico City behind. "Not so far that it can't be driven in a day, but not all the roads will be as good as this one."

"I don't want to push this old pickup too hard, either," Gabriel said. "I know what Pancho told us about how well it runs, but we can't afford to break down."

"It was good to see him and his family again." Cierra leaned back against the seat's tattered upholstery and sighed. "I swear, if Vladimir bothers them, I'll come back and . . . and claw his eyes out myself."

Gabriel laughed. "I believe it. But you shouldn't have to do that. It was just one night. It's pretty unlikely that Esparza will ever connect us with them."

They had hidden the jeep in the shed the night before and pulled the pickup around back to pack the supplies in it this morning. No one in the neighborhood should have been able to get a good look at Gabriel or Cierra, and the chances of Esparza's men even looking for them there were slim.

Pancho and his wife had insisted on giving up their bed for Cierra. Gabriel had slept on a sofa. The house was full of children, but they had all been asleep when the two visitors arrived the night before. That hadn't been the case this morning, when Gabriel had awakened to find four solemn-faced youngsters under the age of five standing beside the sofa and staring at him. He had grinned at them, and that sent them scampering off in search of their *madres*.

The chance to get some rest had helped, and so had the hearty breakfast washed down by several cups of strong black coffee. When they were ready to go, Cierra had hugged Pancho and Pancho's wife and each of their grandchildren and great-grandchildren.

"Why don't you let me come with you?" Pancho had asked. "I know I'm an old man, but I know those jungles down there as well as anyone."

"I'm sorry, Pancho," Cierra had told him. "I couldn't take you away from your family. They need you more than we do."

"I would tell you to be careful . . . but even as a little girl, you were reckless. Always daring to do more and more, even when it put you in danger."

That brought a smile to Gabriel's face when he heard it. His first impression of Cierra had been that she was a beautiful but fairly strait-laced academic and museum administrator. But she had demonstrated since a wilder side. The way she had handled the jeep during the pursuit down the hillside told Gabriel that she had been in some tight situations before.

That was good. He was liable to need a tough, competent ally again before this was over.

But not today. This day turned out to be a welcome respite for Gabriel Hunt. The expressway climbed and wound through the mountains that surrounded Mexico City, then dipped toward the Gulf of Mexico, turning to parallel that body of water several miles inland. The terrain flattened into plains covered by cultivated fields, interspersed with coffee and banana plantations and areas of oil drilling. The driving was easy, as there wasn't too much traffic on the expressway.

Gabriel kept a close eye on the rearview mirror, watching for any signs of pursuit, and he noticed that Cierra often turned around to look behind them, too. Gabriel said, "I'm sorry you had to find out about Esparza like this. I know you considered him a friend."

"Not really," Cierra said. "Not a friend. I appreciated the things he did for the museum, of course, but that was all. We had little in common."

"He claimed to have a passion for history and archaeology."

Cierra shook her head. "I think the only thing Vladimir really has a passion for is power."

"What about money?"

"That goes hand in hand with the desire for power. You can't have one without the other."

Gabriel nodded. Clearly, Vladimir Antonio de la Esparza was going to be a formidable enemy. But Gabriel had gone up against better men than Esparza, he told himself, and he was still here.

They reached Villahermosa late that afternoon and found a rundown motel in which to stay. There were plenty of nicer hotels in the city, but that wouldn't have fit the image of a poor farming couple.

After taking one look at the neighborhood, they decided to carry all of their supplies into the room rather than leaving them in the pickup. As Gabriel slipped the chain into place on the door, Cierra asked, "Were you bored today?"

Gabriel frowned. "What do you mean?"

"No one shot at you all day. That must be a dull day by your standards."

That brought a laugh from Gabriel. "Sometimes my life is as mundane as anybody else's."

"Really?"

"Well . . . sometimes. Not too often."

Cierra smiled. "I think I'll see if the shower works."

She went off into the bathroom, and a few minutes later Gabriel heard the water running in the shower. Through the thin walls, he could hear Cierra turning under its spray, soaping up. He tried to put the image out of his mind; there was still work to take care of. He took off his shirt and removed both flags, which he'd folded and taped to his torso, front and back, in flat, compact bundles. He spread out General Fargo's personal standard on the bed and sat beside it, leaning over to take a closer look at it.

The artwork on the flag was fairly crude and of course somewhat faded, but everything was still clear and distinct. Some of the lines, in fact, were darker than the others, Gabriel realized. The distinction was small enough so that it wasn't likely to be noticed except on close scrutiny. Two such lines made their way in a snaking, parallel path across the hills to the right of the cavalryman figure. Gabriel had assumed at first that those lines just depicted slopes in the hills, but he realized now that wasn't right. In some places the lines cut *across* the slopes that the artist had drawn. They ended at the far right of the circular picture in what Gabriel suddenly realized was a tiny letter *Z*.

No, he thought as his heart began to slug harder in his chest. It wasn't a *Z*. He turned his head so that he was looking at the flag lengthwise, ninety degrees from how it would normally be flown.

It was an *N* . . . for *North*.

The damned thing was a map.

Those two winding lines represented a river making its way generally from north to south. A curving line of right-angled marks crossed the wavy lines, and when looked at from this direction they resembled caret marks . . . which were sometimes used on maps to signify mountains, Gabriel thought. Little squiggles that were meaningless marks one way became smoke from those mountains when looked at the other way.

Volcanoes?

His pulse was racing now. The reason those marks were

slightly darker than the other designs on the flag was because they had been drawn on there *after* the flag was made, after it had been flown in battle, possibly for a number of years. But not any time recently—they were faded by time, too, just not as much. So: Sometime after the start of the war someone had drawn a map on the flag. The most logical person to have done that was the flag's owner—General Granville Fordham Fargo.

But what was it a map to?

He was so engrossed that he almost didn't hear the bathroom door open. He did hear it, though, and glanced up to tell Cierra about his discovery.

The words got stuck in his mouth when he saw that she was standing there in the doorway with nothing on but a towel, wrapped loosely around her torso. Its lower edge fell barely below the curve of her hips, leaving her sleek, honey-golden legs bare. Her arms and shoulders were bare as well, and her raven hair was damp and tumbled loosely around her neck.

Even though the sight of her affected him strongly, it wasn't enough to make him forget what he had found. His voice sounded a little strained, though, as he said, "There's a map."

She stiffened. "A map? What are you talking about?"

"On the flag." He gestured toward it. "Someone drew a map on it. It's hidden in the picture, but if you look closely you can see it."

Cierra hurried forward. If she had intended to seduce him—and the pose she had struck in the bathroom doorway certainly hinted that she had—she had forgotten about doing so as soon as she heard the word "map."

She lowered herself onto the bed next to Gabriel and leaned forward to study the flag. Her eyes followed his finger as he traced the river and pointed out the mountains.

"You can see the letter N when you look at it from this direction," he said, rotating the flag. "That's north."

"Of course," she said with a trace of impatience in her voice. "How could we have missed this?"

"Nobody ever said we were looking for a map. And whoever drew it did a good job of concealing it. Unless you were looking for them, you'd think these were just random marks in the picture."

"But whoever drew it would know where they were."

Gabriel nodded. "That's right."

"General Fargo?"

He shrugged. "Or one of his followers. You can tell from the way the ink is faded that the map wasn't added any time recently. My gut tells me that Fargo either drew it or had someone draw it."

"That's smoke coming from the mountains. They're volcanoes."

"Exactly."

"There are volcanic mountains here in Mexico." A frown appeared on her face. "But the river's not right. You can see the way the mountain range curves around and runs in an east-west direction, while the river bisects it from north to south. The closest area that matches that terrain is—"

"Guatemala," Gabriel said.

Cierra nodded. "Yes. It has to be. The southern tip of Mexico swings to the east to form the Isthmus of Tehuantepec, and that orientation continues on over into Guatemala. The rivers run down from the rain forests to the north into the mountains." She looked up from the map and met Gabriel's eyes. "But what's there?"

He shook his head. "I don't know, but this has to be why Mariella Montez brought the flag to New York. She was going to give it to the Hunt Foundation and ask us to send an expedition down there. I'm sure of it."

"Well . . . in a roundabout way she got what she was after, then, didn't she?"

"I guess you could say that." Gabriel chuckled. "An expedition of one."

"Two," Cierra corrected.

He had glanced down at the flag again, but something about the soft tone of her voice made him look up at her. She had been holding the towel around her, but it had slipped a little, leaving the upper slopes of her breasts uncovered. Gabriel had a good view of the enticing valley between them. It was nicer geography than any you'd find on a map, he thought.

"Two," he agreed as he lifted a hand, slid his palm along her arm and shoulder, enjoying the sleek warmth of her flesh. His hand went behind her head, into that damp tangle of midnight-dark hair, and urged her closer to him. She rested her hands against his chest as their lips met.

That left the towel loose to slide down so that nothing was between them. Gabriel felt his desire growing as the kiss became more urgent. The surroundings were hardly romantic, but that didn't matter all that much when the attraction between two people was strong enough, as it was here.

And at least nobody was shooting at them right now, he thought as he pushed the flag aside so that Cierra could lie back on the bed and pull him on top of her.

Chapter 12

Now that they had a better idea where they were going, speed was of the essence, Gabriel thought. But there was one stop he wanted to make before he and Cierra left Villahermosa and headed south through Chiapas toward Guatemala.

The next morning Cierra made a phone call to the museum. The young man who answered, a graduate student at the university who was interning for the semester, was very upset, she told Gabriel later. Everyone believed she had been kidnapped. Esparza had apparently told the police he had received a ransom demand from the kidnappers, who had first tried to snatch Cierra at the museum and then ambushed her and her escort after they left Señor Esparza's party two nights previously.

Covering his tracks for when she turned up dead, Gabriel thought when he heard about the phony ransom demand.

Cierra had assured Luis, her intern, that she was all right and that she hadn't been kidnapped. The opportunity to lay her hands on a valuable artifact had come up unexpectedly, she told him, so she'd had to leave town in a hurry without letting anyone know where she was going. What she needed him to do was to access the information in the office computer about Enrique Montez, who had sold the Fifth Georgia's regimental battle flag to the museum. Yes, she knew the sale was a hundred years ago. Yes, she realized that the records were incomplete and out of date. She understood how difficult it was, what she was asking. But if Luis could make an effort to track down the Montez family, Enrique's descendants, and find out if they were still in Villahermosa, and if so where they were, that would be a great help, *por favor*. He would be demonstrating his research skills, which would surely put him in good standing for a full-time position after he got his degree. Oh, and if he could keep the assignment strictly confidential, just between the two of them . . .

Gabriel and Cierra waited by the phone, gave Luis the three hours he insisted he would need, and then she called again. He picked up on the first ring and even from halfway across the room Gabriel could hear the elation in his voice. He had the information—what a stroke of luck, the previous director had ordered all the records updated just five years earlier, and this was one of the files that had gotten the full treatment. They had a telephone number for Jorge Montez, the great-great-grandson of old Enrique, who was an executive now in one of the oil companies headquartered in Villahermosa. Or at least he had been five years ago. Cierra thanked him copiously, promised him the earth and sky in terms of reference letters and job prospects, and got off the phone as quickly as she was able, which wasn't nearly as quickly as she and Gabriel would have liked.

Another phone call, this one to Montez's office, gained them the news that Montez still worked there but hadn't gone into the office today. Instead he could be found working from his home, a sprawling mansion with a beautiful lawn that sloped down to the Grijalva River. Gabriel nodded appreciatively as they approached it. So this was what life in Mexico was like if you were an oil company executive.

Not unexpectedly, there were bodyguards at the wrought iron gates leading into the estate, but Cierra had called ahead and spoken to Señor Montez, telling him that she was the director of the Museum of the Americas in Mexico City and that she wished to speak to him about a flag the museum had purchased from his ancestor a century earlier. The bodyguards searched Gabriel and Cierra, looking at them with intense suspicion because of their clothes and the rattletrap old pickup, but it wasn't long before they were shown into an airy breakfast room with large windows overlooking the lawn and the river.

"Dr. Almanzar," Montez greeted Cierra as he stood up from a glass and aluminum table where an attractive, middle-aged woman remained seated. He introduced her as his wife Dolores, then went on, "I am so pleased to meet you." He frowned a little at their clothes, just as the guards had done. "And this is Señor Hunt?"

"That's right," Gabriel said as he shook hands with the man. "From the Hunt Foundation in New York. We're working with Dr. Almanzar on this matter."

"Something about my great-great-grandfather's flag?" Montez asked, still frowning. He was around fifty, with steel gray hair and a neat mustache. "I would not normally have agreed to meet with you on a day when I have so many obligations already, but it is not always that one gets a telephone call about the events of a century ago. This flag you are asking about, it is the one passed down to Enrique by his grandfather Hortensio, the one Hortensio received from the gringo warlord *El General*?"

"That's right," Cierra said. "You know the story?"

Montez said, "It is a family legend, how the American Confederates visited my family's home all those years ago."

"Not this house, though," Gabriel said. "It's not old enough."

"Oh, no," Montez replied with a shake of his head. "At that time my family still had a plantation in the country. That was before oil was found in the region. *El General* and his men rode through there and stopped on their way to wherever it was they were going."

"Tell him about the *tigre*, Jorge," Señor Montez's wife urged.

"Of course, of course, but first . . . would you care to join us for breakfast?"

"That would be wonderful, señor," Cierra said.

When she and Gabriel were settled at the table with plates of food and steaming cups of coffee in front of them, Montez began telling them about the jaguar— because that was what the word *tigre* meant, Gabriel knew.

"In those days the *tigres* still came out of the forest and raided the plantations, carrying off livestock and sometimes children as well. One of old Hortensio's daughters was out riding one day when her horse scented a *tigre* and bolted in panic. The girl was thrown off. She was not hurt badly by the fall, but she would have been easy prey for the *tigre* had not *El General* Fargo come along at that moment. With one shot he killed the *tigre*, even as it leaped at the girl."

"And then they fell in love," put in Dolores Montez, beaming at the romantic turn the story had taken.

"*Sí,*" Montez nodded. "He was older than she by a considerable number of years but still very dashing in his uniform, according to the story. *El General* had stopped at my family's plantation to let his men and horses rest after their long ride from the Rio Grande, but he was determined to go farther south, through the mountains into Guatemala. When he and Hortensio's daughter fell in love, she begged him to stay, but he would not. He said there was a great treasure he sought in the jungles, and that if he found it he would be able to return to his homeland and rebuild the Confederacy." Montez's shoulders rose and fell in an eloquent shrug. "So, since *El General* would not stay, the girl was determined to go with him. They were married, and *El General* made a gift to Hortensio of his battle flag. He said that was all he had to give in return for the hand of the girl."

"Just one flag?" Gabriel asked. "There weren't two?"

Looking puzzled, Montez shook his head. "One flag is all I ever heard about, Señor Hunt. And the story is quite popular in my family. I think if there had been a second flag, I would have heard about it." A look of understanding appeared on his face. "Ah! It is this second flag you and Dr. Almanzar search for, is it not?"

Gabriel and Cierra exchanged a glance, and then both of them nodded. If Montez wanted to think that, it was fine with them. He didn't have to know that they already had the second flag.

"I wish I could be of more help," Montez went on.

"Do you know where exactly in Guatemala the general was headed?" Gabriel asked.

"No. Just somewhere over the mountains."

"Did he have a map, or . . ." Gabriel's voice trailed off as Montez shook his head.

"I do not know. All that was left was the flag, señor, and it was sold by Enrique Montez when hard times had befallen the family for a time."

Señora Montez leaned forward and said, "What about the photo, Jorge?"

"Photo?" Gabriel and Cierra echoed at the same time.

"Ah, *sí*," Montez said. "One of the Americans had a camera. A primitive thing, but it took photographs. I have seen pictures from your American Civil War, taken by the man Brady?"

"Matthew Brady, yes," Gabriel said. "This photographer who was with General Fargo took pictures?"

"One picture. Of the wedding party. Something for Hortensio and his wife to remember their daughter by, you understand, since she was leaving with *El General* and they knew she might never return." Montez shook his head solemnly. "And of course, she never did. No one ever saw her again after she rode off with her new husband and his men."

"Do you still have this photograph?" Cierra asked.

"It is a family heirloom." Montez pushed his chair back from the table. "I'll get it."

Gabriel had no idea if the photograph would be of any help, but it couldn't hurt to take a look at it. Montez went somewhere else in the house and returned to the breakfast room a few minutes later carrying a large, framed photograph. The ornately carved wooden frame looked old, very old. Probably almost as old as the photograph itself, taken more than a hundred and forty years ago.

Carefully, Montez placed the photograph on the table, pushing aside some of the breakfast dishes to clear a space for it. Gabriel and Cierra stood up and moved around the table to get a better look at the picture. Both of them leaned forward to study it.

The photograph had been taken in front of a large plantation house. Dozens of people were crowded onto the long porch that ran from one end of the house to the other, including Confederate soldiers in patched uniforms and whatever other castoffs they could find, and workers from the plantation. In the center of the picture, on the steps leading up to the porch, were gathered the members of the wedding party itself: Hortensio Montez, a stocky man with long, fierce mustaches; his severe-looking wife; a number of other family members; a couple of Confederate officers, the general's best man and groomsman, no doubt; and finally the happy couple, his hand clasped in hers, General Granville Fordham Fargo and the beautiful young woman whom he had rescued from the claws of the *tigre*.

Gabriel suddenly felt like he had been punched hard in the gut.

He recognized General Fargo from the portrait he had seen in the book Stephen Krakowski had shown him at the Olustee battlefield. Fargo looked a little older and more worn-down in this photo, but losing a war would do that to a man. And in this picture he was smiling, as well he might considering that he had his arm around his lovely young bride as she beamed up at him.

The problem was, Gabriel recognized the bride, too.

"Mariella," he said.

"*Sí*, that was her name," Montez said, nodding his head. "Mariella Montez. She was Hortensio's youngest daughter."

You don't understand, Gabriel wanted to say. *I saw this woman three nights ago in New York City.*

"What happened in there?" Cierra asked as they were driving away a short time later. "You seemed like something bothered you a little when you looked at that old photograph."

"If I only seemed a little bothered, then I did a pretty

good job of concealing my reaction." Gabriel took a deep breath. "That was Mariella Montez in the picture."

"Yes, I know," Cierra said, nodding. "She had the same name as the woman who brought the flag to New York. It's not *that* unusual a name, Mariella. Assuming it even was her real name—perhaps the woman in New York merely chose the name as an alias for purposes of meeting with your brother."

"I'm not talking about her name," Gabriel said. "I'm saying it was her. The same woman in the picture. She's the one I saw at the Metropolitan Museum."

Now Cierra looked over at him like he was losing his mind. "But that's—"

"Impossible, I know. But it's true, impossible or not."

"Gabriel . . . you can't mean that. I suppose the woman in New York could have been a descendant of the one in the picture. Perhaps the great-great-great-granddaughter of General Fargo and the original Mariella Montez."

"And looked exactly the same? Not almost the same—exactly?"

"Can you say that with certainty based on a small photograph and a memory of seeing her for just a few minutes several days ago? Maybe the resemblance is not as great as you—"

"Trust me," Gabriel said. "I never forget a face."

"But you can't seriously expect me to believe that she was the same woman. You can't believe it yourself. What would that even mean? Do you know how old she would be if that were true?"

"Yes," Gabriel said.

"And you said the woman in New York appeared to be, what, twenty-one, twenty-two?"

"About that," Gabriel confirmed.

"So you see? It simply can't be like you think."

"It can't be," he said. "But it is."

Nine years ago, Gabriel would have been less inclined to believe the impossible. But that was before the cruise ship carrying his parents on a millennial speaking tour of the Mediterranean had turned up empty, no one on board but three slaughtered members of the crew. All the passengers, three hundred of them, vanished into thin air. It was before his discovery of the tomb of the Mugalik Emperor, in whose airless depths he had encountered a living man, or in any event a speaking one, who had held him at swordpoint for two days and two nights before crumbling to dust when Gabriel tricked him into stepping out into the sun. It was before the events of Christmas 2004, on the Millau Viaduct at midnight, when Giuliana Rivoli leaped naked from the highest mast—a height greater than the summit of the Eiffel Tower—and somehow, impossibly, was found unconscious but unharmed the next morning at its base. *Impossible*, Gabriel had repeatedly found, was often just shorthand for *I don't know how*. There were lots of things he didn't know. That didn't mean they were impossible.

Anyway, right now there was one thing he *did* know.

The answers to all their questions lay over the mountains, somewhere in the jungles of Guatemala.

He floored the gas.

Chapter 13

The highway south of Villahermosa wasn't as good as the one they'd come in on. It shrank from four lanes to two, with no shoulders, and the pavement was cracked and buckled in places. Traffic was sparse. The Mexican state of Chiapas was one of the most dangerous places in the country. Some farming went on there, but the roving gangs that called themselves rebels filled the region, as Cierra had pointed out. Down here in the southernmost part of Mexico, lawlessness was the main industry.

This was where the rusty old pickup would come in handy, Gabriel thought. As long as they were driving it, they wouldn't look like they had much worth stealing.

Cierra didn't say anything more about Mariella Montez, for which Gabriel was grateful. She talked instead about General Fargo.

"According to what Señor Montez told us, the general didn't come down here simply to find a refuge from the Union troops. He was looking for something specific, something valuable."

Gabriel nodded. "Any ideas what it might be?"

"Guatemala was the birthplace of the Mayan Empire," Cierra said. "It spread from there into Chiapas and the

Yucatan. Archaeologists have found gold and jeweled artifacts in the abandoned Mayan cities, but nothing fabulously valuable, at least not that I ever heard of."

Gabriel tugged at his earlobe and then ran a thumbnail down his jawline as he frowned in thought. "Let's assume there really was some sort of treasure that Fargo was going after. How did he hear about it? He was all the way up there in Florida fighting the Yankees."

"Could he have visited Guatemala before the war?"

"I suppose it's possible, but I don't recall seeing anything about a trip to Guatemala in the biographical sketch of him at the battlefield."

"There might not have been a mention of it."

"I got the sense that he was a Georgia boy born and bred; a trip down south for him would've meant Tallahasse or Jacksonville." Gabriel thought about it some more, then said, "I don't think he'd been here before the war. And I think we can assume he drew the map on the flag before he came down here after the war. He'd have chosen some other place to hide it if he'd drawn it after the war ended. Hiding it on the flag only makes sense if he was still using the flag, if it was a natural thing for him to be carrying around with him."

"I suppose," Cierra said.

"And if it was a map of a place he'd never been, he couldn't have drawn it from life or from memory—he must have copied it from another map. Of course, that raises the question of why he didn't just take the other map with him."

"Maybe he preferred a hidden map to one out in the open that someone else could find and steal from him. Maybe he destroyed the other map after copying it onto the flag."

·

"Maybe," Gabriel said. "Or maybe he couldn't take the other map with him for some reason."

"Like what?"

Thinking once more of the Mugalik Emperor's tomb, he said, "It could have been painted on a wall. For instance."

Cierra nodded. "So at some point during the war he found this other map, and he copied it onto the flag, either because he couldn't take the original with him or because he didn't want to. Where does that leave us?"

"In the middle of Chiapas," Gabriel said, "with a hundred-forty-year-old map to follow and no idea what we'll find at the end of it."

As they wound through the mountain passes that afternoon, other vehicles became even more scarce. They saw more mule-drawn wagons and carts than they did other trucks and cars. The road was only intermittently paved, with long stretches of it now being gravel or plain dirt. There were plenty of places where Gabriel could look around and see no signs whatever that they weren't still in the nineteenth century.

That wasn't all that unusual to him, though. He had spent much of his life in far-off, out-of-the-way places where modern civilization was a rumor at best. People liked to think that the entire world had been tamed, that modern technology now reached to all four corners of the globe. They didn't know just how wrong they were.

Bluish gray mountains rose around them as they neared the border crossing from Mexico to Guatemala. Smoke curled from a few of the summits, indicating that those peaks were active volcanoes. They were entering the territory depicted in the map hidden on General Fargo's flag, Gabriel thought. So far they hadn't had any trouble.

Naturally, that couldn't last.

They had just rounded a sharp bend in the road where a steep slope dropped off to the left and another slope rose to the right. Gabriel had to hit the brakes to bring the pickup to an abrupt halt before it ran into an old truck parked across the road. He had time to guess it was a deuce-and-a-half, military surplus, before men came out from behind the rocks at the side of the road and pointed rifles at him and Cierra.

"I knew it!" she said. "I knew we couldn't make it without—"

"Take it easy," Gabriel advised in a low voice. "It's all right to let them see that you're scared, but don't panic. Maybe they'll see that we don't have anything they want and let us go."

"They'll take our supplies, at least."

"We can get more supplies. What matters is coming through this alive."

"Out of the truck, *amigo*!" one of the men said, gesturing curtly with the barrel of his rifle for emphasis. The weapon was probably military surplus, too, but it wasn't a modern assault rifle—not unless you considered a World War I–era bolt-action Springfield modern.

None of the roughly dressed men were well-armed, Gabriel saw as he opened the driver's door and slid out with his hands up. Several of them had old rifles, a few brandished revolvers, and a couple seemed to be armed with nothing more than machetes.

He motioned for Cierra to follow him out the driver's side rather than opening the passenger door. That kept the pickup's body between them and most of the bandits. The steep slope down was at their backs. They might be able to make their way down it if they had to, Gabriel thought, but they'd have to go slowly and could easily be picked off if they tried.

"Come on around here where we can see you," the spokesman ordered. "And don't try anything funny. Keep your hands where we can see them."

"We don't want any trouble," Gabriel said in Spanish as he moved to comply with the command. "My wife and I are going to her family in Guatemala."

The leader of the bandits shook his head. "She don't look Guatemalan." He squinted at Gabriel. "Nor do you. And I don't think you're Mexican, either. I think you're a damn gringo."

Gabriel bit back a curse. He hadn't seriously expected to pass for Mexican, but he knew that the bandits would be even less likely to let them go now that they knew he wasn't. They might think he was a good candidate to hold for ransom, simply because he was American.

"We have food and supplies, and we don't have any quarrel with you," he said. "Take what we have and let us go, and there won't be any trouble."

"Trouble?" the leader repeated. "We're not going to have any trouble. And you're not going anywhere, gringo. Neither is that beautiful wife of yours . . . if she really is your wife."

"Do you know Paco Escalante?" Cierra suddenly asked.

That brought frowns of surprise to the faces of the bandits. "What have you to do with Paco Escalante?" the leader said.

Cierra gave a defiant toss of her head. "Bring me to him, and find out for yourself."

Several of the men crowded around, and they spoke in low, fast tones that Gabriel couldn't make out. He leaned closer to Cierra and whispered out the side of his mouth, "Who's Paco Escalante?"

"The man who murdered my parents," she replied through gritted teeth.

"Oh." Gabriel nodded. "I was hoping maybe he was a friend of yours."

The leader of the bandits stepped forward. "Escalante means nothing. He is an old man. These mountains belong to us now, and we take what we want and do what we please." The rifle barrel centered itself on Gabriel's forehead. "And what I want is to kill you and take your woman, gringo."

In his anger, the bandit had come too close. Gabriel's hand shot out and grabbed the barrel, wrenched it aside before the man could pull the trigger. A shot blasted from the rifle, but it went harmlessly into the ground. Gabriel hauled hard on the weapon, swinging the bandit around when the man refused to let go of the rifle. It wouldn't fire again until somebody worked the bolt and threw another round into the breech.

"Get down!" Gabriel shouted to Cierra as he gave a hard shove and sent the bandit spilling off the road and down the slope. The man yelled curses as he tumbled over and over, bouncing off rocks along the way.

But the man was able to yell, *"Kill them,"* the words drifting up the slope as he kept falling.

The other bandits had hesitated when they saw him fall, and that second of hesitation gave Gabriel time to pull the Colt from his waistband where the old work shirt had hidden it. He went for the men with rifles first, the old revolver roaring and bucking in his fist. One of the bandits doubled over as a .45 slug punched into his belly, and another spun around with a bullet-shattered shoulder.

Gabriel ducked behind the front of the pickup as bullets panged off of it. From the corner of his eye he saw Cierra pick up the rifle the bandit chief had lost hold of before going over the edge. She worked the bolt, and then, lying prone, she fired underneath the pickup. Gabriel heard one of the men scream and figured that Cierra's shot had busted his ankle.

He saw her wince at the pain in her shoulder from the Springfield's kick and roll behind the rear tires to use them for cover. Gabriel popped up and fired over the pickup's hood. The bandits were scattering now as they realized that their intended victims were capable of putting up a fight. Another of them went down as a slug from Gabriel's Colt tore through his thigh.

A rattle of rocks behind him warned Gabriel that the stocky, bearded leader had finally stopped his tumble down the mountainside and was climbing back up again. The shooting had drowned out the sounds of his efforts until it was almost too late. As Gabriel spun around he saw the man lunging at him, machete held high. The blade swept down in a killing stroke calculated to cleave Gabriel's head to the shoulders when it landed.

Gabriel didn't let it land. He fired twice at almost point blank range, the bullets smashing into the bandit's chest and knocking him backward. He tumbled down the slope again, but probably didn't feel the bruising impact this time since Gabriel was pretty sure both rounds had gone into the man's heart.

"Gabriel!" Cierra cried raggedly. "The others!"

Gabriel spun around again. Only four bandits were left, but that was four too many, considering that his Colt was empty now. The men charged, firing as they came. Bullets smacked into the pickup, shattering glass and punching holes in metal.

"Throw me the rifle!" Gabriel yelled to Cierra over the racket, and she tossed it in his direction. He caught it, knowing that they were going to be overrun before he could get off more than a shot or two. He worked the bolt and came up out of his crouch, ready to fire through the broken windows of the pickup's cab.

Instead he held his fire when he saw the four bandits twisting in midair as bullets ripped through them. Flesh exploded and blood sprayed in the air. One after another the men flopped into the road before they could reach the pickup. Gabriel saw their bodies continue to jerk for a moment as more bullets thudded into them.

Then the shooting stopped, and as always after a battle, the silence that settled down possessed an eerie quality, as if you might hear departed souls singing their death songs if you listened hard enough.

Cierra still lay on the ground behind the rear tires, her arms crossed over her head. Slowly, as the silence descended over the mountainside, she lowered her arms and lifted her head to look around.

"Gabriel?" she said, as if amazed that they were both still alive. "What . . . what happened?"

"Somebody else opened fire on those bastards and finished them off," Gabriel explained.

"But who?"

"Offhand, I'd say it was those guys," Gabriel replied as he looked up the slope and saw that half a dozen men had emerged from behind some rocks higher up. They were as roughly dressed as the bandits had been, and if anything, their weapons looked even older and more time-worn.

But however old they might be, those rifles and pistols had worked well enough to shoot holes in the bandits who had been about to kill Gabriel and Cierra. And Gabriel was grateful for that . . . although he had a sneaking suspicion that their situation hadn't improved much.

His suspicion was confirmed a second later when Cierra stood up, brushed herself off, and looked at the men coming down the slope. A horrified expression appeared on her face. "*Dios mio*," she said in a husky whisper.

"You know them?" Gabriel asked.

She nodded. "The big man in the lead . . . that's Paco Escalante."

She swallowed hard and repeated what she had told Gabriel a few minutes earlier, not that he had forgotten.

"The man who murdered my parents."

Chapter 14

Gabriel didn't know if the bandit camp was still in Mexico or over the border in Guatemala. Not that it mattered one bit in this wild territory. Borders meant little here, and governments were far away. The only power that mattered was the power of the man next to you holding a gun. In this case, that was Paco Escalante, and what mattered was that he hadn't ordered his men to kill them . . . yet.

They'd been taken, at gunpoint, to what looked like a semipermanent camp, with crude, thatch-roofed huts instead of tents. Gabriel and Cierra were stashed in one of the huts until Escalante could decide what he wanted to do with them.

"Do you think he knows who you are?" Gabriel asked.

She shook her head. "He hasn't seen me for many years. I've changed enough since then that I don't think he recognized me. He, on the other hand, hasn't changed at all."

Escalante was a tall, gaunt man with a salt-and-pepper beard and a mat of silvery hair. His face was weathered and lined from years of living mostly outdoors, much as

Pancho Guzman's had been. Escalante's men were cut from similar cloth, all of them older, still plenty tough but with an air of weariness about them, as if they had been fighting the same fight for too long.

Gabriel and Cierra had been forced to climb into the back of the pickup with the supplies and ride there while one of Escalante's men drove and another sat with them, his gun aimed casually in their direction. They left the highway, such as it was, and followed what appeared to be little more than a goat track deep into the jungle that covered the lower slopes of the mountains. Clearly the bandit knew where he was going, because even though the goat track disappeared, he found a way through the jungle and was able to keep the pickup moving.

When they reached the camp and stopped, Escalante had the two prisoners placed in the hut, with armed guards on either side of the entrance, and they had remained there ever since. The fading light that came through cracks in the rough walls told Gabriel that the day was drawing to a close. It would be night soon.

And who knew what dangers the darkness might hold?

"Can you tell me a bit more about what happened on your parents' plantation?" Gabriel said. "I know it's painful for you, but it's important." Cierra nodded. "You said you'd seen Escalante before."

"He worked on the plantation at one time. He and my father always got along well. Escalante was even his assistant foreman for a while. But then his wife grew ill and died, and he became very bitter. Didn't show up for work, wouldn't come out of his room. Eventually he just walked off. Word came back that he was living as a bandit. It was difficult for my father—he'd considered Escalante a friend. But he rebuffed every effort my father made to contact him.

"At least he left the plantation alone, though—spared it from his raids. I imagine it was because my father had always treated him fairly. But he was not the only bandit in Chiapas, and my parents decided it was too dangerous for me to stay on the plantation. They sent me away to school . . . and while I was gone, a group of bandits attacked. They killed my parents and burned the house and all the crops—it was done with exceptional viciousness. The police later found out it was Escalante's gang that did it. I could never understand why."

"Maybe to prove to his men that he wasn't soft," Gabriel said. "Maybe he was taking heat for leaving your father alone for so long. Or maybe he just snapped, lashed out at anything that reminded him of his wife's death."

"Or maybe he is simply the monster people say he is."

"Then why did you ask those other bandits if they knew him?"

"I was desperate—it was the only idea I had," Cierra said. "They were going to kill us. And I thought, if they're part of his band, he might show pity on me because of what he'd done to my parents so long ago. And if they were part of someone else's band and thought we had a connection to him, maybe they'd be afraid to hurt us . . ."

"Well, no one's hurt us so far. Though I don't know how long he plans to let us live. Or how long until allies of the other band decide to come after him for revenge. That fellow made it sound like Escalante's not a feared man in these parts anymore."

Before they could continue the discussion, a step sounded outside the hut and the door swung open. Escalante's figure loomed in the doorway with the fading light behind it.

"Come out, you two," he ordered.

Gabriel and Cierra were sitting on the ground. Gabriel got up first, unkinking muscles that had grown stiff, then took Cierra's hand and helped her to her feet. As they stepped out, Escalante moved back, staying well out of reach with the experience-honed wariness of a feral animal. Two men with rifles flanked him. Two more moved in from either side and prodded the prisoners toward a large cleared area in the center of the huts.

The twilight had a greenish tint to it from the trees and vine-covered brush that surrounded the camp. The scene might have been beautiful in a wild, untamed way if they hadn't been waiting to find out if they were going to live or die, Gabriel thought.

"First of all," Escalante said as he faced them in the clearing, "who are you?"

"We had a farm, but we lost it because of the taxes," Gabriel said. "We were going to stay with my wife's family in Guatemala—"

Escalante stopped him with a casual wave of the hand. "Don't waste your breath and my time, *amigo*. You're an American, and this woman is no farmer's wife, no matter how she's dressed." His eyes narrowed as he stared at Cierra. "In fact, there is something familiar about her—"

"Look, if you let us go, I can make it worth your while," Gabriel cut in.

The bandit leader looked amused. "Oh, you can, can you, *amigo*? Just how will you do that?"

"I can raise some ransom money. Not a lot, you understand, but enough that it ought to buy our freedom. All I need to do is get in touch with the American embassy in Mexico City—"

"A man who drives a pickup so old and rusty it's about to fall apart?" Escalante shook his head. "No, I think not. I think you're some sort of American gangster, come down here to take advantage of my people."

"Then why did you save us from those bandits?"

Escalante leaned over and spat in the dirt. "Because I have no use for that pig Gomez and his men. They thought they were the most feared band in these mountains, but they learned to their regret that they were wrong. You and the señorita just happened to be there, señor. We weren't saving you . . . we were killing them."

"Well, either way, we appreciate it. And if you let us go, we'll appreciate it even more."

Cierra said, "Gabriel, I think I should—"

"Don't," he snapped, knowing what she was about to reveal.

"A wise man listens to his woman, my friend," Escalante said with a smile. "But then if you were a wise man, you wouldn't be here, now would you?"

"Just tell me what it will take to buy our freedom."

"Buy?" Escalante shook his head. "One cannot *buy* freedom." He held up a finger. "One can only *fight* for it."

"Then let me fight for it," Gabriel said and Escalante's eyes narrowed. "You saw us fight Gomez—I killed him, not you. If there's a fight you need help with . . ."

"I need no gringo's help," Escalante spat. "But if you are so eager to fight, we can oblige you." He turned and used his outstretched finger to make a crooking motion. "Tomás."

Gabriel had a bad feeling about this. He turned and saw the group of bandits that had surrounded them parting to allow a man through into the clearing.

The newcomer was several inches shorter than Gabriel but considerably wider as well. His long arms were almost as thick as the trunks of young trees, and his shoulders strained at the olive-drab fabric of the old fatigue shirt he wore. He was mostly bald, with only a fringe of gray hair around his ears. Not a young man by any means, but still tough and dangerous, Gabriel judged. Perhaps even more dangerous than if he had been young, because he'd have the skill and guile of a veteran.

"Let's see how you fight, gringo. You shall be our evening's entertainment," Escalante said. "And if you can defeat Tomás, well . . . we'll *talk* about your freedom."

"Talk?" Gabriel said. "I want your word. If I win, you'll set us free."

Escalante laughed. "Where in life do you see guarantees, *amigo*? The only guarantees in this world are of pain and suffering, and death at the end. All else is a gamble."

Gabriel's mouth tightened. Even as Cierra's hand clutched at his arm, he knew he couldn't turn down the bandit leader's offer, no matter how tenuous it was.

"All right," he said. "I'll take the gamble."

"Gabriel . . ." Cierra began.

"It's okay," he told her as he turned to her and smiled. "He doesn't look so tough."

"Let me—"

He shook his head before she could go on.

"You refuse to let your woman intercede for you?" Escalante said. "I would expect no less of a true man."

Gabriel turned back to him. "What do we fight with? Pistols? Machetes? Or a good old-fashioned bare knuckles brawl?"

"None of those," Escalante said with a shake of his head. "Bullwhips."

Tomás grinned.

"Bullwhips?" Gabriel repeated.

All the bandits were grinning now. One of them went into a hut and brought out a couple of coiled whips of plaited leather.

"Oh, Gabriel!" Cierra threw her arms around his neck and hugged him hard. In his ear, she whispered, "I tried to warn you, you fool! I remember hearing about Tomás when I was a little girl. He can take out a man's eyes with a whip! He'll cut you to ribbons!"

Gabriel reached up to stroke her hair as she embraced him. "It's all right," he whispered. His mouth was dry, but not too dry for him to add, "I learned to use a bull-whip when I was a boy. An old friend of my father's taught me."

"A friend of . . . ? Wasn't your father some sort of Classics professor?"

"Trust me," Gabriel said.

He let go of her and stepped back, then reached out to take the whip that was offered to him. His fingers closed around the long handle. It was made of wood with strips of leather wrapped around it. With a flick of his wrist he shook out the whip itself, made of more long strips, braided together. It coiled and writhed at his feet like a snake.

"Oh, ho, Tomás," Escalante said. "It looks like our American friend has held a whip before."

Tomás spat, and if ever such a gesture could be eloquent, this one was. His contempt was obvious. He snapped his wrist, and the whip he held leaped into the air like it was alive before jumping back with a sharp crack that sounded like a gunshot.

Gabriel could have cracked his whip, too, but he didn't see any point in showing off. He had probably done a little too much of that already, just by not feigning awkwardness when he was handed the whip.

"If you survive this, *Gabriel*," Escalante said, using the name Cierra had called him, "then you deserve to live."

"Then this is a fight to the death?" Gabriel said.

Tomás spoke for the first time, in a voice like ten miles of gravel road. "For you it is."

Cierra reached for Gabriel again, but Escalante took hold of her arm and pulled her back before she could get to him. The rest of the men backed off as well, giving Gabriel and Tomás plenty of room in the middle of the clearing.

Once they started swinging those bullwhips, they would need the room.

Tomás struck first, lashing out with the whip. Gabriel had seen the flare of anger in the man's eyes and the bunching of the muscles in his shoulders, and that was all the warning he needed to leap aside. As he moved he snapped his wrist and sent his whip darting toward Tomás. The stocky bandit was incredibly fast for a man of his bulk, though. Gabriel's first strike missed just as Tomás's had.

Tomás drew his whip in and began to circle slowly, forcing Gabriel to circle as well. Then with a grunt he attacked again, this time going for Gabriel's legs. Gabriel tried to dart out of the way, but the very tip of the bullwhip struck his calf and left behind a line of fiery pain when it snapped back. Gabriel glanced down and saw that the whip had sliced right through his jeans.

Tomás rushed him then, snapping the whip high overhead. If the weighted tip caught him in the eye, it would be over, Gabriel knew. He flung up his left arm, felt the vicious bite of the whip against his flesh as it cut through his sleeve.

Holding his right arm down low, he flicked his wrist and sent his whip leaping out again. It slid in underneath Tomás's guard and cut the bandit across his belly. Tomás howled in pain and anger but didn't pause or stop pressing his attack. Gabriel spun to one side and cracked his whip. This time it struck Tomás's thick left thigh and drew blood.

Gabriel was vaguely aware of the other bandits yelling encouragement to Tomás. From the corner of his eye he caught a glimpse of Cierra standing beside Escalante, her face twisted with lines of fear. She was saying something, but he couldn't take the time to make it out, because Tomás was coming at him again.

Gabriel watched the man's arm swing back, gauged where his whip was aimed, and then swung his own to meet it, the lengths of braided leather meeting in midair, twining around one another. Gabriel yanked fiercely, hoping to pull the handle out of Tomás's hand, but the stocky man held tight, pulling back mightily and almost overbalancing Gabriel, who stumbled forward. He caught himself with his free hand, the fresh cut on his forearm stinging. With his other hand, he swung the whip handle in a tight circle, desperately trying to untangle his whip from Tomás's. He saw the other man doing the same, and after a second the two whips slid apart. Each man drew his in, eyeing the other warily.

Tomás raised his arm and with a practiced flick shot the leather at him. Gabriel ducked under the slashing whip and suddenly drove forward, burying the top of his head in Tomás's bleeding gut. He pushed with all the strength in his legs and knocked Tomás backward. The bandit lost his footing and fell, crashing down hard on his back.

Gabriel landed on top of him, planting a knee in Tomás's belly. Tomás was red-faced and gasping from the fall. Gabriel didn't give his opponent the chance to catch his breath. He made a loop with his whip and twisted it around Tomás's neck, then scrambled around behind the bandit to tighten the noose, twisting with the wooden handle to turn it into a makeshift tourniquet. Grunting with the strain, Gabriel rose to his feet, lifting Tomás with him and making the whip sink deeper and deeper into the flesh of the man's neck.

Tomás flailed with his free hand, swinging behind him, but the blows he landed didn't reach Gabriel with enough force to do any damage. Not so the bullwhip in Tomás's other hand, which danced and weaved around Gabriel, snapping and popping and bloodying him in half a dozen places. His thick work shirt was swiftly sliced through and his back would have been as well, had it not been for the extra padding of the regimental flag hidden beneath his shirt. But the whip cut cruelly into his sides and shoulders, landing for an instant, then moving on to strike again somewhere else. Gabriel ignored the pain and hung on, planting one knee in the other man's back for leverage.

He had held his own in the contest so far, but he knew if he gave Tomás enough chances the man would eventually kill him.

This fight had to end here and now.

As Gabriel gritted his teeth and looked over Tomás's shoulder, he saw several of the bandits pointing guns at him with angry expressions on their faces. They didn't like seeing their *compadre* on the brink of defeat, and at the hands of a gringo, at that.

But Paco Escalante motioned for them to lower their weapons, and grudgingly, the bandits did so. After what seemed like an eternity, Tomás stopped fighting. His muscles went limp, and the bullwhip slipped from his nerveless fingers. Gabriel didn't think the bandit was shamming. Tomás wouldn't have let go of his bullwhip if he were still conscious. Instantly, Gabriel let off on the pressure he'd been exerting with his whip and allowed Tomás's ungainly form to slump to the ground at his feet.

If ever the other bandits were going to shoot him, it would be now.

Escalante motioned his men back, though, and came forward, bringing Cierra with him. He gestured toward Tomás, who lay there out cold but still breathing, and said, "You did not kill him. It was supposed to be a fight to death."

Gabriel was a little out of breath himself. "Didn't see . . . any need to," he said.

Escalante reached to the holster on his hip and drew a revolver from it. "You seek to gain favor with me by sparing one of my men when you could have killed him?" The gun rose to point at Gabriel. "You think I know mercy? That may have been the worst mistake you ever made, *amigo* . . . and the last."

Gabriel was ready to make an exhausted desperation leap at the bandit leader, but Cierra got between them.

"Stop it!" she cried as she stood there trembling with anger, her fists clenched at her sides. "You murdering bastard! Do you want *me* to fight for our lives now? I'll fight! I'll fight anyone you say, and I promise you I won't hold back from killing him!"

Gabriel muttered, "Oh, hell." But then he saw a sudden flare of recognition in Escalante's eyes. A shadow spread slowly across the bandit leader's craggy face.

"My God," Escalante murmured. "Cierra Almanzar." He lowered his gun. "You know, I believe you would fight, at that."

Gabriel heard the metallic ratcheting of guns being cocked all around them.

But then Escalante made another gesture, telling his men to hold their fire. He looked at Cierra and said,

"Your father's death, your poor mother . . . can you ever forgive me?"

Then he put his arms around a shocked Cierra and held her as tenderly as if she were his own daughter as tears ran down his leathery cheeks.

Chapter 15

"I'll never forget, even as a child you had that fiery temper," Paco Escalante said. It was a short time later and he sat with Gabriel and Cierra on logs next to a campfire. Night had closed down completely over the mountainous jungle, but the flames kept a small part of the darkness at bay. Escalante went on, "That is how I finally knew who you were. I saw that temper on display more than once when I worked on your family's plantation."

Despite the primitive setting, Escalante had a modern first-aid kit, and one of his men had crudely disinfected and bandaged the cuts left on Gabriel's shoulders and legs by Tomás's bullwhip, after first tending to Tomás's own wounds.

Escalante had given them food and drink, too, from their own provisions, which the bandits had appropriated from the back of the pickup in the name of the *revolución*.

Gabriel didn't know if they were still prisoners or not, and he wasn't going to press the issue just yet. Not having guns pointed at them was already an improvement in their situation.

Escalante went on, "Those were the good days, before everything went wrong."

"If you want my forgiveness, as you claim," Cierra said, "you must tell me how my parents died."

Escalante nodded. "It was not at my hands, Cierra, this I swear. It was not my wish that any harm befall them. In fact, I didn't even know about the raid on the plantation until it was too late to stop it. There was a member of my band, a lieutenant of mine, who was an ambitious man. He thought he should be *el jefe*, not me. He said that I was too gentle with the landowners, too weak to drive them out. So, while I was away negotiating with a man for some weapons, this lieutenant convinced the other men to go with him and attack the plantation. I returned too late to stop them. By the time I got there, your mother and father were . . . already dead. The buildings were in flames."

It was a touching story, Gabriel thought, but there was no way of knowing whether or not it was true.

On the other hand, Escalante *had* spared their lives, and as far as Gabriel could see, the bandit leader had no reason to do that unless he really did want to make amends.

"At first I didn't believe that you had killed them," Cierra said. "But then all the reports said that it was your men who attacked the plantation. I came to hate you for what you had done. What I *thought* you had done."

A pained expression crossed Escalante's face. "For this, I am sorry, *señorita*. If I could go back and change things, I would. But this is a power granted to no man. The clock winds one way only." He rested his hands on his knees. "Now, you must tell me why you and this man have come to Guatemala. You risk your lives traveling through this area—it must be a very important matter."

"We are trying to find out what happened to someone

who disappeared in this region many years ago," Cierra explained. "Many, *many* years ago. More than a hundred and forty."

"I am old, *señorita*," Escalante said with a smile, "but I am not *that* old."

"He was an American," Cierra went on. "A soldier, a general in the Confederate army during the American Civil War. His name was Fargo."

Escalante shook his head. "I know nothing of this."

Cierra explained briefly about the general's pilgrimage down from Mexico, although she didn't mention the flags that were once again securely hidden under Gabriel's shirt. When she was finished, Escalante nodded solemnly and said, "I remember hearing stories about this gringo warlord, but I never knew his name. You seek to find out what happened to him?"

Cierra nodded. "That's right."

"And others are trying to stop you?"

"So it appears." Cierra hesitated. "A man named Esparza, most likely."

"Vladimir Antonio de la Esparza?"

"You've heard of him?" Gabriel said.

"Just because we live in the rain forests and the mountain jungles does not mean we are completely cut off from the outside world, Señor Hunt. We hear news from time to time. Señor Esparza is a rich man, therefore a famous man." Escalante frowned at Cierra. "He is also said to be a ruthless man."

"I think that is right, Paco," she said. "He has tried several times already to have us killed."

"I would help you fight him," Escalante declared, "as partial payment of the debt I owe you, but . . ." He lifted his hands and spread them. "Look around you. My men and I may fight like *tigres*, but we are gray now and there are not many of us left. I fear we would not be much help against a man such as Esparza."

"That's all right," Cierra said. "I'm just glad that I finally found out the truth, after all these years."

"*Sí*. And I can promise you safe passage through the mountains to wherever it is you are going."

"We haven't quite figured that out yet," Cierra admitted.

"When you do, we will accompany you. In the meantime, you can use the hut where you were kept earlier."

Gabriel wondered if that was the bandit leader's way of telling them they were still prisoners.

"You are free to go whenever you wish," Escalante went on, as if reading Gabriel's thoughts. "I would advise you not to leave without taking us with you, though. These mountains are full of peril."

"I remember," Cierra said. "Thank you for your hospitality, Paco."

Escalante shook his head. "It is the least I can do, señorita."

Cierra got up and went to the hut. Gabriel stayed where he was for a moment, to give her some privacy, and he said quietly to Escalante, "What happened to that lieutenant of yours, the one who went against your wishes and led the attack on the plantation?"

A sad smile curved Escalante's lips. "What do you think happened to him, Señor Hunt?" He drew the machete that was sheathed at his hip and ran the ball of his thumb along the keen edge of the blade.

Gabriel nodded. "I see. In my country, there's a saying, when a subordinate makes a mistake, about how 'heads must roll.' But it's only a saying."

"Your country," Escalante said, "has the luxury of sayings."

Cierra was waiting for Gabriel when he got back to the hut. She rose from the crude bunk and said, "Get your shirt off."

"What, no foreplay?" Gabriel said with a grin.

"We've got to look at that flag again. The one with the map."

He stripped his shirt off, wincing as it brushed his cuts, and tossed it on the bunk. Cierra helped him untie the strips of cloth that held the flags in place on either side of his torso. The regimental flag, which had been against his back, had been sliced through in multiple places by Tomás's whip, but General Fargo's personal standard had been safe against his chest. They spread it out now and studied it in the light of the hut's single lantern.

Gabriel's finger traced the lines that marked the course of the river. "We'll have to ask Escalante if he can figure out what river this is."

"I can tell you that already, from the way it's oriented in relation to the mountains. It has to be the Black River. It flows from the mountains up into the rain forests, then makes its way across to the Caribbean. You just can't see that on this map."

"You're sure?"

"Trust me," she said.

Gabriel smiled and leaned closer to the flag. "Too bad the old boy didn't draw a big red X on here to mark the spot where he was going," he muttered. "That would have been a big help." He frowned and put a finger on the flag. "Unless he did . . ."

Cierra studied the small, black-rimmed hole in the fabric that Gabriel was pointing to. "A bullet hole. Hardly surprising considering that this flag went through a battle. There are several holes like that in the other flag."

"There are holes, but not like this one," Gabriel said. "Look at that dark ring around it."

"Some sort of smudge. In all these years, there's no telling what sort of dirt got on it."

Gabriel shook his head. "I don't think that's dirt. I think that's a burn. A powder burn. The hole is smaller, too. A ball from a musket didn't make it. I think somebody held a small caliber weapon, maybe a derringer, right up to the flag and fired a shot through it. That wouldn't have happened in battle, and it's not likely it happened by accident, either."

"Then you're saying . . ."

"I'm not saying, I'm asking: What if that hole is our big red X?"

Gabriel saw excitement spark in Cierra's eyes. "You think General Fargo fired that shot to mark his destination?"

"Who would think twice about a bullet hole in a battle flag? But there it is, right in the middle of that wider space between two of the mountains."

"A valley," Cierra whispered.

"That'd be my guess."

"It could be," she said. "It could."

"And since there's nothing else on the map that could . . ."

Cierra nodded, convinced. "The question is, how can we get there." She bent closer, counted markings on the flag with her finger. "It's one, two, three mountains past the river." She looked up at Gabriel. "That's about five days' travel from here on foot, maybe two on horse-back."

"What about the pickup? I'm not sure Escalante's going to give it back to us, but . . ."

Cierra shook her head. "There are no roads fit for such a vehicle."

"I guess we'll have to put our hands on some horses, then."

"Escalante will know where to find some," Cierra declared. "And he feels he owes me."

"He does," Gabriel said, "but don't overestimate his altruism. If he comes with us, he's liable to want a cut of whatever it is the general was after, assuming it's still there."

"So let him have a cut. Do you begrudge him that, Gabriel? If he helps us?"

"We don't even know what it's a cut of. Whatever it is might not even be there anymore."

"We have to assume it is," Cierra said. "General Fargo never went back to the States with the treasure he was after. And your mysteriously youthful Mariella Montez wouldn't have come to New York with that flag and set off all the fireworks if she didn't think there was something still there to find. And a man like Esparza wouldn't be so anxious to get his hands on something unless it was pretty valuable."

Gabriel nodded. "But they might all be wrong."

"In that case, Escalante will get a cut of nothing. And so will the Hunt Foundation. But if there is something to find, we'll all get a piece of it. We need all the help we can get, Gabriel. You're an impressive man, but you can't do it alone. We have to risk letting Escalante help us."

Gabriel knew she was right. It was a risk, indeed, trusting a bloodthirsty old bandit like Escalante. But they had come too far and been through too much danger to turn back now. If they were going to find out the secret of the mysterious valley that lay there in the mountains, beyond the Black River, they would have to take the chance.

Chapter 16

Gabriel woke up with an armful of warm, nude, female flesh, which almost made up for the fact that he was lying in a narrow bunk with nothing but a thin, bug-infested mattress for cushioning in a crude hut in the middle of the Guatemalan mountains. Cierra stirred sleepily against him. Her hand rested on his chest, and even though he didn't think she was fully awake yet, it began sliding down over his belly toward his groin.

Gabriel would have encouraged her to continue that exploration if not for the fact that he heard footsteps coming toward the hut. They stopped right outside the door, and Paco Escalante called, "Cierra? Señor? I have news."

Cierra came awake the rest of the way and sat up, taking the threadbare blanket with her and holding it over her breasts. "Gabriel?" she said, her voice a little fuzzy with sleep. "What time is it?"

"Morning, looks like," Gabriel replied as he swung his legs out of the bunk and stood up. Except for the ragged bandages from last night, he was as naked as Cierra was, and the light that came in through the cracks in the hut's walls threw slanting bands of illumination across his body. The effect looked better on her, he thought as she threw the blanket aside, stood up, and reached for her clothes.

"Just a minute, Paco," she called to Escalante.

They had been allowed to bring in some of the supplies from the pickup. Instead of the peasant blouse and long skirt she had been wearing the day before, Cierra pulled on khaki trousers and shirt and a pair of boots. Gabriel tied on the flags, fore and aft, and then dressed in a pair of tan pants and a blue shirt. They left the hut and went to see what Escalante wanted.

The bandit leader greeted them with a smile. "You both slept well, I hope?"

"Reasonably," Cierra said, and Gabriel asked, "You have news?"

Escalante nodded. "*Sí.* I have contacts all over the country, and a short time ago I received word of another group of travelers passing through the mountains not far from here. They have three trucks and many supplies and weapons. My men would like to ambush them."

"What business is this of ours?" Cierra asked.

"They also have a prisoner with them, my scout reports. A young woman. A *beautiful* young woman."

"Mariella?" Gabriel said.

Escalante shrugged. "Perhaps. My source did not know her name. There is only one way to find out for certain. But when I heard about this prisoner I thought of the woman you told me about, the one taken by men working for Vladimir Esparza."

"Esparza's had her all this time," Gabriel said. "He's probably been trying to force her to reproduce the map for him. If he's coming here, it means he was finally able to break her and get the information. Now he's trying to get there ahead of us."

Cierra looked at Gabriel. "You can't be sure it's her.

You can't even be certain that these men work for Esparza."

"Señor Escalante's men want to ambush the convoy either way," Gabriel said.

Escalante nodded. "This is true."

"I will go with you," Gabriel said.

"If you're going, I'm going," Cierra said.

"It will be dangerous," Escalante warned. "We will be outnumbered. But we will have the advantage of surprise, and the terrain will favor us if we can get ahead of them and meet them at a spot of our own choosing."

"Can we?" Gabriel asked.

Escalante grinned. "No one knows these mountains better than I do, Señor Hunt. We can get around them on horseback and set up an ambush."

"Let's do it, then," Gabriel said.

"And what if you're wrong about who it is?" Cierra said.

"We'll burn that bridge when we come to it," Gabriel said.

They ate breakfast in the saddle. It had been a while since Gabriel had been on a horse, and it felt good to be riding again. You didn't get to ride much growing up in New York City, but over the years he had visited a lot of places where a good horse was the best means of transportation, and Paco Escalante and his men had some fine mounts.

Gabriel didn't ask himself where the bandits might have gotten those horses. Some things it was just as well not to know.

"You look like you've ridden before," he commented as he looked over at Cierra, who swayed slightly in rhythm with her horse's gait.

"Every day, when I was a child," she replied. "My father always said I could ride before I could walk."

"You're not the girl I took you for when I first met you."

She snorted. "I should hope not. You, however, are exactly the sort of man I took you for."

She kneed her mount gently and rode off. Gabriel followed close behind.

Their encounter at the museum seemed like more than two nights earlier, he thought. He wondered how Michael was doing back in New York. It didn't seem likely that Esparza would have any reason to go after him at this point, but Gabriel hoped he was keeping a low profile nonetheless.

Escalante led the group, which numbered fifteen not counting Gabriel and Cierra. They followed a trail that left the jungle behind and climbed high into the mountains. The path hugged the side of a slope that fell away dizzyingly on one side and rose to smoking volcanic peaks on the other. They would be in trouble if one of those sleeping giants decided to erupt, Gabriel knew. But it was one more thing they couldn't do anything about, and Gabriel put it out of his mind.

"Careful," Escalante called over his shoulder. "It's a long way down."

"I can see that," Cierra said. "Don't worry about me."

"I'm not. I'm worried about that fine horse you're riding, señorita."

She laughed. She was directly behind Escalante now, with Gabriel behind her and the rest of the men strung out along the mountainside.

Tomás was directly behind Gabriel. He had caught the thickly built bandit glaring at him several times. Gabriel wasn't too happy with having Tomás at his back, but that's where *el jefe* had stationed him and that's where he rode. Escalante had explained to all fourteen men that Gabriel and Cierra were under his protection, and Gabriel was fairly confident Tomás wouldn't go against his leader, not while Escalante had his machete at his hip. But it was a possibility Gabriel couldn't dismiss entirely.

The air was crystal clear, the sky a beautiful blue. Despite the hazards, Gabriel found himself enjoying the ride. But the enjoyment was short-lived. After climbing for about an hour, the trail began dropping again. Gabriel suddenly spotted a road far below them, and along that road crawled three trucks.

Esparza's convoy, he thought. It had to be.

He pointed them out to Escalante, who claimed to have already seen them. "Can we still get ahead of them?" Gabriel asked.

"This trail will allow us to reach the Black River bridge before them," Escalante said. "That's where we will stop them."

From behind Gabriel, Tomás called, "Will we blow up the bridge?"

"Then we could not use it if we needed to, *amigo*," Escalante replied patiently. "We will find another way."

They followed the steep, winding path downward until they came to a stream spanned by a sturdy-looking, one-lane wooden bridge. The bridge was about fifty feet above the water, which raced along at a good clip and bubbled over its rocky bed.

"The Black River," Escalante announced. "Listen."

Gabriel listened and heard the grumble of truck engines coming from the west. It was hard to tell how far away the convoy was, but Escalante seemed to think they had plenty of time. He didn't appear to be in any hurry as he gave his orders.

They led the horses across the bridge and then hid them in a stand of trees on the far side of the river. Escalante picked out eight men to conceal themselves around the western end of the bridge. He went to the eastern end with the rest of the men. Gabriel and Cierra crouched in a clump of boulders near the road as the bandits spread out, using rocks and brush for cover.

"My men will open fire when the trucks are in the middle of the bridge," Escalante explained. "They will shoot out the tires on the lead truck and the one bringing up the rear, trapping the one in the middle as well. Then the men in the trucks will have no choice but to surrender, because we'll be able to pick them off if they try to get off the bridge."

"You've used these tactics before," Gabriel guessed.

"Multiple times. And why? Because they work," Escalante said. "My men are nearly always outnumbered and we are rarely as well armed as our enemies. But they are the best shots in the mountains and know no fear, and between that and our tactics we have survived."

"You think I could have my Colt back?" Gabriel asked.

Escalante grinned and pulled the weapon from behind his belt where he had tucked it. "I do think so," he said as he handed the gun to Gabriel. "Your rifle is over there on one of the horses. You have time to get that, too, if you want."

"I'll use it," Cierra volunteered. "I can handle a rifle."

Gabriel hurried over to the horses, got the Winchester and a box of ammunition, and moved in a crouching run back to the boulders where Cierra and Escalante had hidden. The trucks' engines were louder now. The convoy would reach the bridge within minutes.

Gabriel handed the Winchester to Cierra. She worked

the lever to jack a round into the chamber. Her expression was grim and a little scared, although she appeared to have her fear well under control.

"I want the prisoner," he said to Escalante. "If they're Esparza's men, I don't care what you do with the rest of them."

"That will all depend on whether or not they want to surrender the trucks and everything they hold. If they are willing to trade a long walk back to civilization for their lives, we will let them go."

Gabriel didn't really expect that to happen and didn't much care. He just wanted to get Mariella away from her captors before all hell broke loose.

The lead truck came into view around a bend about two hundred yards from the bridge. One by one, the other two vehicles followed it, and all three of them lumbered toward the Black River. Gabriel worried for a moment that caution might lead whoever was in charge to order that the trucks cross one at a time, but they had no reason to fear a trap.

The truck rumbled out onto the thick planks of the bridge. The span was long enough so that fifty yards still separated the lead truck from the eastern end of the bridge when the vehicle bringing up the rear was fifty yards from the western end.

Escalante had drawn a bead with his rifle. When he fired, it was the signal for his men to open fire as well.

Shots roared out from both ends of the bridge. Cierra joined in, aiming at the tires on the lead truck. The driver of that truck slammed on his brakes as one of his front tires exploded. The truck veered sharply toward the flimsy railing along the side of the bridge.

Gabriel held his breath. If the truck went through that

railing and plunged into the river, everyone in it might die in the crash or be drowned by the fast-moving stream. He had no way of knowing if Mariella Montez was one of the passengers.

The driver was able to bring the truck to a stop a couple of feet short of the railing. Its other front tire had burst now from the bullets ripping into it, and the truck slewed diagonally across the bridge as it came to rest, blocking the narrow span completely.

The driver of the truck in the rear had thrown his vehicle into reverse and tried to back off the bridge. He must have guessed what the bandits were trying to do. He was too slow, though. Bullets shredded his rear tires, and the truck ground to a halt on its wheel rims.

They had the convoy pinned down, Gabriel thought. Now all they had to do was get the men in the trucks to surrender.

That wasn't going to be easy. Men with rifles leaped from the canvas-covered backs of the vehicles, took cover between them, and opened fire in both directions.

Escalante's men were too well hidden, though, to be taken in the fusillade. Like phantoms they darted from rock to tree to bush, so that the men trapped on the bridge never knew where the next shot was coming from. Individual shots, quiet and sure, picked off the men from the convoy; one by one they dropped their rifles and sprawled on the bridge planks to lie motionless in death.

After a few minutes of fierce firing on both sides, the shots began to die away. An uneasy silence settled over the bridge. Escalante took advantage of the respite to shout, "You on the bridge! Do you hear me?"

"We hear you!" a harsh voice came back.

"If you want to live, release your prisoner! Allow her

to walk off this end of the bridge! Then throw your guns down and walk to the other end! Leave the trucks and everything in them, and you can have your lives!"

"Go to hell!" the spokesman for the trapped men bellowed back, and as soon as the words were out of his mouth, the shooting started again.

The air began to grow hazy with gunsmoke as the fighting continued for several minutes. Most of the shots came from the men in the trucks. The bandits held their fire for the most part, not wanting to waste ammunition and taking a shot only if it presented itself clearly to them. Two more men on the bridge fell, blood welling from the wounds they had suffered.

"Hold your fire! Hold your fire!"

The command came from the leader of the men on the bridge. Gabriel was eager to get a look at him. He wanted to know if he was the same ugly, broken-nosed bastard, the one Gabriel had bayoneted in Florida.

"You want the girl? You can have her!"

Suddenly, Mariella Montez stepped out from behind the lead truck. Gabriel recognized her instantly, just as he recognized the man who emerged right behind her and pressed the barrel of a heavy revolver against her head. His right arm was in a sling, but he seemed to be handling the gun in his left hand just fine. Old Broken-Nose, all right, the son of a bitch.

"Gabriel Hunt," the man shouted. "I know you must be here somewhere."

Cierra glanced over at Gabriel in surprise. Gabriel shrugged.

"I don't know who your allies are," Broken-Nose went on, "but your stamp's all over this." The man had a faint accent, Slavic, perhaps, or Russian. What he was doing here in the middle of Guatemala, Gabriel didn't know. Perhaps Esparza recruited killers from all over the world, selecting the worst of the worst.

"Do you want me to try to pick him off?" Escalante asked quietly.

Gabriel shook his head. "Not with that gun to Mariella's head. No matter how good a shot you are, we can't risk him pulling the trigger."

Mariella was no longer dressed in the evening wear she had sported in New York. Now she wore nondescript fatigues like the men. But she still managed to look beautiful in them, somehow, despite the look of fear etched on her face. Seeing her in person again, even from this distance, Gabriel was more convinced than ever that she was the same woman in the wedding photo he had seen in Villahermosa. Impossible or not.

He raised his voice and called, "You know you're surrounded. We can kill every one of you, or we can let you live. It's up to you."

Broken-Nose laughed. "I knew you must be behind this, Hunt!"

"All you have to do," Gabriel shouted, "is let the woman go."

The man shook his head and kept the gun pressed to Mariella's temple. "Oh, no," he said. "If you want her so bad . . . you come and get her, Gabriel Hunt."

Chapter 17

Cierra clutched Gabriel's arm as he started to stand up. "You can't go out there!" she said. "They'll kill you!"

"No they won't," Gabriel replied. "That won't gain them anything except a quicker execution. These aren't ideologues, they're professionals. They don't want to die. They'll negotiate if they think that's what it takes to get them out of this alive."

"You don't really believe that, do you?"

"Well, we'll find out."

Escalante said, "I'll have the *bastardo* in my sights the whole time, Gabriel. If he takes the gun away from Señorita Montez's head and points it at you, I will kill him in the blink of an eye."

"You do that," Gabriel agreed. He kissed Cierra quickly, then moved out from behind the boulder where the three of them had taken cover. He wrapped his right hand tightly around the butt of the Colt Peacemaker that hung at his side.

His skin crawled a little as he walked out onto the bridge. Fifty yards away stood his broken-nosed nemesis with the gun still pressed to Mariella's head. Gabriel strode toward them. From this angle, he couldn't see the other gunmen crouched behind the trucks, but he could feel their rifles trained on him.

He came to a stop about ten yards from Mariella. "All right, I'm here. Let her go."

"Why should I do that?" the man asked with a sneer. "Now I have both of you in my power. I can kill you both before anyone can stop me."

Gabriel shook his head. "You won't kill either one of us. Señor Esparza wouldn't be happy with you if you did."

"Oh? And why is that?" He didn't bother to deny that he worked for Esparza, Gabriel noted.

"You need Señorita Montez," Gabriel said with a nod toward Mariella. "She might not have told you the truth about where you're going, not the whole truth. And because she might not *ever* tell you the whole truth, you need me alive. Because I do know where your destination lies."

The man frowned. "You try to confuse me with talk. But my orders are clear. I am to kill you, Gabriel Hunt, wherever and whenever I find you." He raised his voice in a shout to his men. "Use the machine guns! Kill them all!"

Machine guns? That didn't sound good.

But Gabriel didn't have time to worry about that threat, because the man jerked the gun barrel away from Mariella's head and swung it toward Gabriel, leaping aside as he did so. He must have figured that at least one rifle was aimed at him. Escalante's weapon cracked, but the bullet whipped past Gabriel and missed his enemy as well, smashing into the hood of the lead truck.

Gabriel raised his gun, but he couldn't shoot without endangering Mariella. He plunged forward instead, ducking as the man fired his big revolver. Gabriel felt the wind-rip of the slug's passage past his ear as he left his feet in a diving tackle that sent him crashing into both Mariella and her captor.

As they fell he caught a glimpse of men throwing aside the canvas on the back of the truck to reveal a belt-fed .50-caliber machine gun mounted on a swivel so that it could fire either over the top of the truck's cab or back behind the vehicle. With a chattering roar it began spitting lead toward the rocks and brush where Escalante and his men were hidden. Cierra was over there, too, in the middle of that deathstorm, but there was nothing Gabriel could do to help her.

He had his hands full.

The collision had knocked Mariella free from the man's grip. All three of them fell against the truck's front bumper. Broken-Nose slashed at Gabriel's head with the revolver. Gabriel ducked so that the blow landed on his left shoulder just inches from one of the cuts from Tomás's whip. His arm went numb for a moment. He swung his own pistol at the other man's head, but the man avoided the blow, grabbed Mariella again, and shoved her hard against Gabriel. She fell against his chest and both of them went down.

"I'm so sorry," she said.

"We'll talk about it later," Gabriel said, sliding out from under her.

Snarling with hate, Broken-Nose jerked his gun toward Gabriel, who couldn't stand up without risking getting his head chopped off by the machine gun fire. He grabbed Mariella and rolled instead. Broken-Nose's revolver roared twice. Splinters leaped up and stung Gabriel's face as the bullets slammed into the bridge planks. He did the only thing he could. He tightened his grip on Mariella and kept rolling.

Right under the railing and off the side of the bridge.

Mariella screamed as they plunged toward the river. Gabriel hung on to her and managed to turn their bodies so that they would hit the water feetfirst. He hoped the river was deep enough so that they wouldn't break every bone in their bodies when they landed.

Despite the tropical climate, the streams that flowed through these highlands were cold, so the chilly water packed a breathtaking shock as Gabriel and Mariella plunged into it. They went under, deep. But their descent had slowed by the time Gabriel felt the rocky stream bed under his booted feet. He kicked off against it and sent them back toward the surface.

The swift current had them in its grip, sweeping them away from the bridge. As they broke the surface and Gabriel hauled air into his lungs, water geysered around them from bullets splashing into the river. Broken-Nose was still up there on the bridge shooting at them.

"Got your breath?" Gabriel shouted to Mariella. When she nodded, he added, "Well, hold it," and went under again. Their clothes and boots helped hold them down as the current carried them along.

Gabriel kept them underwater until Mariella began to writhe and struggle in his arms. He figured she wouldn't be able to hold her breath much longer, so he headed for the surface again. When they came up this time he saw that the current had carried them around a bend in the river. The bridge was no longer visible behind them.

"Hang on to me," he told Mariella. "I'll try to get us to shore."

"I can swim," she insisted.

Gabriel let go of her. The current was too strong for them to swim directly to shore, but they were able to angle in that direction and slowly make their way closer to the east bank as the river carried them along. Finally, they both grabbed vines that dangled from overhanging tree branches and pulled themselves onto dry land again.

As Gabriel lay there breathing heavily, he listened to the diminishing sounds of gunfire. The battle between the bandits and Esparza's men seemed to be just about over. He didn't know who had won . . . but the overpowering advantage the machine gun conveyed didn't make him optimistic about the outcome.

Concern for Cierra gnawed at him. Even though she'd had good cover with Escalante, that machine gun had thrown so much lead that they would have been in considerable danger from ricochets alone. And those .50-caliber slugs would chew right through the brush where some of Escalante's men had hidden. The odds, not in the bandits' favor to start with, had gotten a lot worse once that big gun opened up.

But there was nothing he could do about that now, Gabriel told himself. He had his own worries, such as being stranded in the middle of the Guatemalan jungle with Mariella . . . and with only one gun. He was thankful he'd been able to hang on to the Colt, and he still had a box of ammunition in his pocket. Once the revolver dried out, it ought to work. It had been through worse.

If Broken-Nose and his friends had survived—and Gabriel had a feeling that was likely—they would come looking for him and Mariella. The two of them needed to get moving. He sat up and asked her, "Are you all right? Were you hit during all that shooting?"

She was breathing heavily, too, and it took a moment before she was able to struggle into a sitting position and give Gabriel a weak nod. "I'm fine," she said. "I wasn't hit."

"How about before? Do you have any injuries from when Esparza and his men interrogated you?"

"How do you know about Esparza?"

"A friend introduced me to him. Hopefully you'll get to meet her." *If she's still alive.* Gabriel thrust the thought away. "I knew he was involved because he matched the description of a man who'd come to the Olustee battlefield looking for information about General Fargo."

She nodded as if what he'd said made perfect sense to her.

"Esparza tried to make me talk," she said. "But I didn't care what he did to me. I wasn't going to betray my people." A bitter tone came into her voice as she added, "In the end it didn't matter. He found out what he needed to know another way."

That statement puzzled Gabriel, but now wasn't the time to probe deeper. He got to his feet. "We'd better get moving. We need to get away from the river before that bastard comes looking for us."

"Podnemovitch," Mariella said. "That's his name. Alexei Podnemovitch. He's some sort of distant cousin to Esparza. I think Esparza's mother was Russian."

Always good to put a name to a face, Gabriel thought. Even an ugly face.

He took Mariella's hand and helped her to her feet. Heading east, they started into the thick jungle that lined the river.

Vines curled around their feet and brambles clung to their clothes, slowing their progress through the vegetation. Gabriel kept a close eye out for snakes. The birds that would normally be singing in the trees were quiet now, startled into silence by the thunderous gunfire that had filled the canyon just minutes before.

"Did you get the flag?" Mariella asked after a few minutes' slow progress.

"The one you brought to New York? Yes, I have it, and the Fifth Georgia's regimental flag as well."

"The other flag isn't important. What about the water?" Her voice caught a little. "Was . . . was any of it left?"

"You mean the water that was in that old whiskey bottle?" Gabriel shook his head. "Sorry. It all spilled when the bottle broke."

Mariella winced. "I was afraid of that. Your brother didn't think to try to collect any of it and have it analyzed?"

"We had other things on our minds. Should we have?"

"It would have been better if you had. The water was more important than the flag, although the flag does show the location of Cuchatlán."

"Cuchatlán," Gabriel repeated. "What's that?"

"My home."

He heard the wistfulness in her voice and would have asked her to tell him more about it, but at that moment he heard men's voices coming from somewhere close by. He stopped short and held up a hand in a signal for Mariella to halt as well.

They stood there, motionless and silent, and listened for a moment. The voices were coming closer, so Gabriel motioned Mariella toward a jutting rock face covered with vines. She hurried over to it, grabbed hold of the vines, and started climbing.

The bluff was about ten feet high. When Mariella reached the top, she flattened on the surface and reached a hand down toward Gabriel. He realized she wanted him to toss the gun up to her. He did so, carefully. If it fell and discharged, the shot would bring Esparza's men on the run.

Mariella caught the revolver's barrel, and the ease with

which she turned the Peacemaker around and wrapped her fingers around the walnut grips told Gabriel she had handled a gun before. While she covered him, he grabbed the vines and scrambled up the rock face.

He stretched out next to her and they waited. What they did next would depend on how many men were searching for them.

After a few more minutes of crashing through the brush, two men pushed their way into view. Each was carrying a rifle. Gabriel had held a slim hope that the searchers might turn out to be Escalante's men, but he didn't waste time being disappointed. He and Mariella held their breath as the men moved past beneath them.

Mariella still had the Colt. They would be a lot better armed, Gabriel reflected, if they could get their hands on those rifles. He tried to communicate by gestures what he planned to do, and was satisfied that Mariella understood. He also pointed to the gun and shook his head, so she'd know not to fire unless it was absolutely necessary.

Silently, Gabriel came up on his hands and knees and then pushed into a crouch at the edge of the bluff. Neither of the men had glanced in this direction yet, but they started to look up just as Gabriel launched himself off the bluff. One man had time to yell, but the shout was cut off as Gabriel crashed into him feetfirst.

Both of the men were bowled over by the impact, the first one knocking over the second. Gabriel landed beside them. One of the men had lost his rifle, but the other had held onto his weapon and tried to swing the barrel toward Gabriel. He grabbed it and twisted it aside, wrenching as hard as he could. The man's finger, caught in the trigger guard, broke with a sharp snap. He opened his mouth to scream, but Gabriel drove the rifle butt into his face before he could. He collapsed—unconscious or dead, Gabriel didn't know which.

That took care of one of them, but the other chose this moment to tackle Gabriel. They rolled on the ground as they struggled, smacking forcefully into the bole of one tree after another and getting whipped in the face by the underbrush. Esparza's man wound up on top, reached back, and slugged Gabriel hard with a right cross to the jaw, then another. Rearing up, the man pulled a machete from a sheath at his waist. The blade hung in the air, poised to come sweeping down in a blow that would chop Gabriel's head cleanly from his body.

Chapter 18

He threw up his hands to block the other man's swing, but as he did so, Gabriel heard a whistling sound in the air. Something wrapped around the would-be killer's hand before the machete could fall, jerking the man's arm backward as he grunted in surprise. A rustle of leaves, the flicker of sunlight on a blade . . .

And Gabriel saw the man's head topple from his shoulders to bounce once and roll a couple of feet away. His expression was still surprised, not pained. There hadn't been time for that.

The headless corpse swayed on top of him. Gabriel shoved it away. As the body thudded to the ground beside him, Gabriel looked up into the craggy, grinning face of Paco Escalante. The machete in the bandit leader's hand had cut through the man's neck so cleanly and swiftly there was hardly a smear of blood on the blade.

"It appears we found you just in time, Gabriel," Escalante said as he reached down to take Gabriel's hand and help him to his feet. "Heads must roll, eh?"

Gabriel wiped the back of a hand across his mouth and then nodded. That was about as close a call as he could remember. "Yeah. I appreciate it, Paco. You, too,

Tomás," he added with another nod to the burly bandit who was unwrapping his bullwhip from the wrist of the dead man.

Gabriel looked around. Escalante and Tomás appeared to be alone.

"Is Cierra . . . ?" he asked.

"I'm up here, Gabriel," she called from the top of the bluff. Relief flooded through him at the sound of her voice. He looked up and saw Cierra standing next to Mariella.

Gabriel turned his attention back to Escalante. "And the rest of your men?"

The bandit leader's face became grim. "Perhaps some of them on the other side of the river got away. I do not know. But of the ones on this side, we are all that is left."

"I'm sorry, Paco," Gabriel said, and meant it. The men had been bandits, had probably been responsible for a great deal of death and suffering over the years. But he wouldn't be here without their help, and neither would Cierra or Mariella.

"When you live a life such as ours," Escalante said, "you don't expect to die in bed with your great-grandchildren around you. At least we accounted for quite a few of them, too. Unfortunately, there were just too many. And they had those devil guns."

"They have more than one machine gun?"

Escalante nodded. "There was one mounted on each of the three trucks."

"Podnemovitch came armed for bear."

"Podnemovitch?" Escalante repeated with a frown.

"The big, broken-nosed son of a bitch who's in charge of that bunch. Tell me he was one of the ones you took down."

Escalante shook his head as Cierra and Mariella began

climbing down the vines from the top of the bluff. "He lives," Escalante said. "But he is not the man in charge. I saw him taking orders from another man. Tall, lean, gray hair."

"Esparza's with him," Cierra said as she reached the ground beside them. "I saw him, too, Gabriel."

"Really? Esparza himself?" Gabriel said. "I wouldn't have expected him to come down here. It's pretty far from the world of mansions and cocktail parties."

"That tells us how important this is to him," Cierra said.

"Of course it's important," Mariella said. "I assure you it's the most important secret in the world. Any man would come in person to see it. Any man."

Gabriel ached to find out more about this important secret, starting with just what it was, but with Podnemovitch and the rest of Esparza's men searching both sides of the river for them, there was no time to stand around and talk. Instead the five of them began working their way through the jungle away from the stream. When they reached a jutting shoulder of the mountain that formed the eastern side of the canyon, Mariella took the lead.

"I know every trail and hiding place in these mountains," she said. "We must reach Cuchatlán before Esparza and his men, so that we can warn my people."

It took what was left of the morning to reach a safe place where they could briefly rest. Mariella led them to a pass high on the mountain and then down the far side into an even narrower canyon. Empty stomachs began to remind them that it had been a long time since any of them had eaten. They had taken the two rifles carried by Podnemovitch's men with them and had several weapons of their own, but they couldn't risk any shots to bring down game because of the noise. A swift throw of Tomás's machete caught a brightly plumaged bird in midflight, though. In a matter of minutes he had dressed out the bird and had it roasting on a sharpened stick over a small fire.

There wasn't much meat to the bird and it didn't taste particularly good, but Gabriel ate hungrily anyway as he hunkered on his heels along with the others. In this wild setting, they might well have been members of some prehistoric tribe . . . except for the rifles and pistols, of course. He and Cierra had cell phones, too, for all the good they did. No signal reached into these remote mountains, and Gabriel's phone probably hadn't survived its dunking in the Black River. He didn't bother digging it out to check.

And though they couldn't pause long enough for an in-depth discussion, they were able to speak briefly, in a hushed undertone in case their pursuers were in earshot.

Mariella said, "Esparza and his men won't be able to travel much farther by road. They'll have to abandon their trucks and go ahead on foot, like us. But we're a smaller group. We can move faster and reach Cuchatlán before they do."

"That's the third time you've mentioned this place," Gabriel said. "What is it?"

"The birthplace of the Mayan Empire," Mariella said.

Cierra frowned at her. "Mayan?" She shook her head. "That's impossible. There are no signs of Mayan civilization in this area."

Mariella just smiled, as if she knew better. She got to her feet and said, "We must go."

Cierra gave Gabriel an exasperated look. He shrugged. It was doubtful that they could force Mariella to talk until she was ready, and anyway, they had to keep moving if they wanted to get where they were going before Esparza and his men.

It took the rest of the day to reach the next pass through the mountains. Mariella led them along a narrow ledge that twisted along the heights. They came to an overhang that formed a cavelike recess in the face, and she said, "We can camp here tonight. No one will be able to see a fire if we build one here."

"What will we do for food and water?" Cierra asked.

Mariella gave her a slightly superior look. "Why do you think I chose this place? My people use it sometimes when they're hunting."

She went to the back of the cave and returned with a couple of canteens and something wrapped in a piece of hide. She unwrapped the bundle to reveal strips of jerked meat that she passed around. Gabriel wasn't sure what sort of meat it was—monkey, he suspected—but under the circumstances he wasn't complaining. It tasted all right when he washed it down with the water from one of the canteens.

In the fading light, he studied the canteen and frowned. The letters CSA were stamped into it. He looked up at Mariella and asked, "Confederate States Army?"

"That's right."

"This is a museum piece. A century old. It might even be valuable."

"It *is* valuable. It holds water when you are thirsty. How much more valuable can a thing be?" She moved off to tend the fire. The altitude wasn't high enough here for the temperature to get very cold at night, but there would be a definite chill in the air before morning.

"Now," Gabriel said as the five of them sat at last, resting their aching legs, "I think it's time that you tell us what this is all about, Señorita Montez."

Mariella hesitated a moment before answering but finally nodded and said, "You deserve to know, Señor Hunt. All of you do. As I mentioned earlier, Esparza is after the greatest secret ever discovered."

"Which is . . . ?" Gabriel said.

"The secret of eternal life," she said simply.

Gabriel thought of the Ponce de Leon signs in St. Augustine. "You mean like the Fountain of Youth?"

"Exactly," Mariella said with a smile. "Only in our language we call it the Well of Eternity."

After a couple of seconds of looming silence, Cierra said, "Oh, come on! You can't be serious."

Mariella's face flushed with anger. Gabriel said, "Let's hear her out."

"Thank you, Señor Hunt," Mariella said with a frosty glance toward Cierra. "I knew I could trust you to keep an open mind, considering some of the expeditions the Hunt Foundation has been involved in."

"I'm not saying I believe you," Gabriel said. "Not yet. But I want to hear what you have to say."

"Very well. Not far from here, in our valley, lie the ruins of the Mayan city Cuchatlán. It was from here that the Maya began to spread out three thousand years ago and establish their empire."

"The Mayan empire," Cierra said, "was located in Chiapas and the Yucatan. I spent a year conducting research in the ruins of Chichén Itzá. The jungle swallowed it up after it was abandoned, and it was lost until about a hundred and eighty years ago, but in its time it was the center of the Mayan empire."

Mariella nodded. "It was—in its time. But Cuchatlán was the center of the empire long before Chichén Itzá. And the jungle swallowed it as well. But even covered by the jungle, its great secret was still there, a well fed by an underground stream that rises from springs in the mountains. Whoever drinks the water from the Well of Eternity . . . lives forever."

"You're going to have to give us more of an explanation than that," Gabriel said.

Mariella smiled and nodded. "Many centuries ago, Mayan explorers left this land to venture out into the Gulf of Mexico, taking barrels of the water from the Well of Eternity with them to sustain them as they started a colony in what is now Florida. They had a wanderlust, a desire to explore; some say it was inspired by visitors who had traveled across the seas and stayed to make their home with the Maya.

"Only a small amount of the water is needed to reap its benefits. Once a year the Maya of Cuchatlán would hold a ritual, a religious ceremony, passing around a cup from which each adult drank, from the oldest to the youngest. A few sips are enough to restore youth and vigor for the coming year. The explorers were able to take enough of the water with them to keep them young and healthy for centuries."

Cierra looked like she wanted to call the story hogwash, but Gabriel made a patting-the-air gesture in her direction and she remained quiet.

"To store the water they brought with them," Mariella went on, "when they reached Florida and found a place where they wanted to settle, they built a rock-lined pool, and before filling it they etched a map to their home on the pool's bottom."

"The Fountain of Youth," Gabriel said.

"Some called it that, when rumors spread. The Maya never did."

"And what happened to this . . . pool?" Cierra said,

unable to hold her tongue any longer. "Or are you saying there are still ancient Maya living in Florida today? Perhaps in one of that state's famous retirement communities?"

"No," Mariella said. "There are no Maya living there any longer. The water was enough for centuries—but not forever, and eventually it ran out. That's what they'd put the map there for, to remind them how to return and get more. But none of the expeditions they sent ever came back—perhaps because there was no longer a city here for them to return to. And without a new supply of the water, the Mayan colonists resumed aging normally. In time they died. But their bloodlines continued, in the local Indians with whom they had intermarried. And the rumors continued, of the Fountain of Youth, even after there was no more fountain and no more youth to be had. Ponce de Leon heard of it and came to the New World seeking it, only to find it gone. But the legend remained, and some people have sought the truth of it ever since."

"Like General Fargo?" Gabriel said.

"Yes. Perhaps you know that he was a professor of natural science before the war. He discovered the pool built by the Mayan colonists while he and his cavalry regiment were serving in Florida. He heard the legends from an old, old Indian living near the site, who'd heard them from his own grandfather, who'd heard them from his. He explained that the markings on the rocks were supposed to be a map—a map leading to the true Fountain of Youth, though of course he called it the Well of Eternity. Granville made a rough copy of the map, hiding it within the drawing on the flag, and made plans to find Cuchatlán after the war."

Mariella sounded a little sorrowful as she went on, "As

it happens, artillery fire during the battle of Olustee destroyed the pool, so the map copied onto the flag was the only one still in existence. That flag is the one I brought to New York. We wanted to give it and a sample of the water from the Well to the Hunt Foundation."

"Why us?" Gabriel asked.

"We are not so isolated as you might think—we make a point of gathering news of the outside world. And we thought your foundation would understand what he had discovered and would be able to convey the secret responsibly to the outside world."

Cierra looked like someone who had finally taken all she could stand. " 'We thought'!" she burst out. " 'We wanted'! You and 'Granville'! You speak of General Fargo as if he were still alive!"

"But he is," Mariella said. "He is my husband."

Silence descended on the group.

"I knew it," Gabriel said. "You're the woman in the picture."

"Picture?"

"A photograph of your wedding party that your great-great-great nephew—hell, there'd be more greats than that, but you get the idea . . . a photo he showed us in Villahermosa. You were standing on the steps of your father's plantation house with the general, and all your family and his men were gathered around you."

A wistful smile curved Mariella's lips. "I remember that day so well. It was a good day, a happy day, even though I knew I would be leaving my family forever. I'm glad the photograph has survived for all these years and my family has not forgotten me. It will sound foolish to you, I'm sure," she continued, "but it feels like it could have been yesterday, or last year. Rather than a century or more."

Escalante and Tomás wore blank expressions. They had been listening to Mariella's story, too, and clearly didn't know what to make of it, but also weren't inclined to get in between the two women.

Cierra looked back and forth between Gabriel and Mariella and said, "You're both insane."

"What's so insane about it?" Gabriel said. "When people came from Europe to America at the turn of the last century, their lifespans increased, and their children's even more. Why? Diet, among other reasons. Surely you're not doubting that there are things you can swallow that make you healthier or live longer—I'm sure you've visited a pharmacy or two in your day."

"Longer, sure. But not centuries."

"Why not? There's research going on right now into extending human lifespan—mitochondrial research, telomeric research, and don't ask me what any of that means because I don't know, but I do know we've funded some of it and Michael's convinced it's not quackery. Not all of it anyway."

"That's sophisticated genetic engineering," Cierra said stubbornly, "not drinking water from a well."

"Sometimes," Escalante said, clearing his throat first, "the oldest ways turn out to be the best."

"No. No—I will not accept a fairy tale about people living hundreds of years!"

"All right," Gabriel said. "You don't have to. All you have to accept is that other people have accepted it—starting with Mariella here and ending with Esparza out there somewhere in the jungle with his machine guns. Even if it's all myth and no substance, there are men willing to kill over it. Men who *have* killed over it. Men who have tried to kill us."

That silenced Cierra's objections.

Gabriel turned back to Mariella. "So you're saying that this Well of Eternity was the great secret beyond the mountains that General Fargo was looking for, the one he thought would help him restore the Confederacy. And I imagine it would have. Face it, if he possessed the secret of eternal youth, he could have gotten the backing of any nation on Earth. And you're saying he did possess it. So why didn't he carry out the rest of his plan?"

"It took us months to find the Well. They were not easy months, and they opened his eyes to a great many things. When we got here, he'd begun having second thoughts, and after he'd stayed a while . . . his plans changed. He no longer wanted to reignite a war. He no longer wanted hatred to divide his homeland." She smiled. "And as he likes to say, he was selfish. He had found paradise, and he had no desire to leave."

"Then why send you to New York now?"

"Word had somehow gotten out; rumors were starting to spread once more. We'd had more than one persistent explorer come close to discovering us—more in the past two years than in the prior twenty. These were people who would have stolen the secret for themselves; people who would have destroyed everything we had built. We could fight off one, two, perhaps more—but eventually would come the one we couldn't fight, and then what would become of the Well?

"Granville believes that the answer is not more secrecy but, at long last, openness. That the scientists in your employ could have the water analyzed to see if it might be possible to determine what gives it its remarkable powers. If it could be duplicated, then the Hunt Foundation could perhaps administer a program to make the water available to all nations—and could also protect the source, so that our life in Cuchatlán could continue undisturbed. I was to give the sample of the water to your brother for that reason; I brought the flag with me to help convince him of the truth of my story."

"Michael can be a skeptical little rascal, all right," Gabriel said with a smile.

"Perhaps he's simply not as gullible as his brother?" Cierra suggested.

Gabriel didn't take offense at her tone. She was a scientist, after all. And she hadn't seen some of the things he had.

Gabriel tugged at his earlobe as he thought about what Mariella had told them. After a moment he said, "Why did Esparza send Podnemovitch and his men to stop you from handing over the water and the flag to Michael? How did he even find out all this in the first place?"

A pained look passed over Mariella's face. "The people of Cuchatlán were betrayed," she said. "One of our representatives who went into the outside world to gather news decided to try to make himself rich by selling our secret. He found out that Esparza has funded research into prolonging human life—perhaps you and he have even funded some of the same undertakings. And this man, Hector, thought that Esparza would be a likely buyer. Unfortunately for Hector, he did not know how truly ruthless Esparza is."

"He told Esparza the whole story?"

Mariella shook her head. "Not at first. He realized that if he told Esparza everything he knew, Esparza would have no reason to keep him alive. Hector only told him enough to pique his interest—and then fled south and hid. Esparza sent one group of men to search for him while another investigated the partial story he had been told."

"That must've been when he and Podnemovitch went to Florida," Gabriel said.

Mariella continued, "Unfortunately, one of the things Hector *had* told Esparza was that Granville planned to send me to New York with the water sample and the flag. I reached New York before Esparza's men could stop me, but Podnemovitch followed my trail and as you know he made it to the Museum in time to intercept me."

"Podnemovitch didn't get the water or the flag, but he got *you*," Gabriel said. "And he saw the bottle destroyed, the water lost. He must have figured we weren't likely to make sense of the markings on the flag—but just to be safe, Esparza left Podnemovitch behind to make sure we didn't interfere with his plans." Gabriel grinned. "Which shows he doesn't know me very well. I'm not so easy to kill—and when anyone tries, it makes me curious to find out why."

Escalante said, "Does trouble always follow you so diligently, *amigo?*"

Gabriel chuckled. "Not always. Just most of the time." He turned back to Mariella and asked, "How does Esparza know where he's going now, if you didn't tell him? We know he doesn't have the flag."

"His men finally located Hector and brought him back." Her face darkened with anger. "This time he told Esparza everything he knows. Esparza gave him no choice. He beat it out of him. I saw some of it. It was truly terrible.

"He's keeping Hector alive in case he needs any more information from him, although I don't know what else Hector could tell him. We were prisoners for a time in the same cell, and then later the same truck. That's how I learned about his involvement in this affair. He confessed to me one night, half boasting, half begging for forgiveness. I told him I'd never forgive him, that none of us would. That his folly had doomed us all. He still seemed to harbor notions, even after everything he'd gone through, that Esparza might let him live, might even reward him. It's madness." Mariella leaned back, sipped from one of the canteens. "Does that answer all your questions, Señor Hunt?"

"For now," Gabriel said.

"And do you believe me?"

"I believe you believe. As for me . . . I guess you could say I'm reserving judgment."

Cierra snorted. Mariella gave her an icy glance and then said, "You will all see the truth for yourselves when we reach Cuchatlán."

The fire had burned low, and shadows filled the cave-like area. The faint light from the flames was a reddish gold glow burnishing the faces of Mariella and Cierra and the two men. It made the men look older, Gabriel thought, but the women—it made them both look more beautiful, if such a thing was possible.

He had heard some astonishing things tonight—things most people would scoff at or dismiss. Cierra clearly felt that way. And maybe she was right.

But maybe she wasn't.

Certainly Esparza thought she wasn't.

Either way, it was as Mariella had said: The truth was waiting for them, somewhere out there in the night, in the lost valley of the Mayas.

Chapter 19

When Gabriel woke in the morning, his muscles were stiff from sleeping on the floor of the cave, which had only a thin layer of sand over hard rock. He stirred a little and became aware that there was soft warmth pressing against both sides of his body. He had gone to sleep between Cierra and Mariella, and as he opened his eyes he saw that Cierra had shifted so that she was snuggled up next to him with her back to his chest. Mariella must have moved around some during her sleep, too, because she was pressed against him from behind, with an arm draped over his hip.

Gabriel couldn't help but grin as he lay there between the two women. On the other side of the cave, Escalante and Tomás were shivering under their coats. He could almost hear his brother's voice in his head: *Only you, Gabriel, could find yourself stuck in a cave on the side of a Guatemalan mountain and still wind up spending the night between a pair of beautiful women.*

Of course, one of those women was well over a hundred years old, Gabriel reminded himself, and a married woman to boot. That is, if Mariella's story was true.

He moved a little more and that woke up Cierra, who

let out a soft groan as she stretched. Then she seemed to become aware that she was spooning with Gabriel and pulled away slightly as if she were embarrassed. She looked around, saw Mariella cuddled against Gabriel from behind.

"She didn't waste any time, did she?"

"Hey, she's an old married lady," he said. "Really old."

"Doesn't seem to have bothered you."

Mariella's hand, meanwhile, lifted from his hip, curled into a fist, and punched him on the shoulder, showing that she was awake and had heard what he'd said.

"Years don't matter in Cuchatlán," she said. "And don't flatter yourself, Señor Hunt."

"Wouldn't think of it," Gabriel said as he sat up.

Escalante grinned at him. "You slept well, Señor Hunt?"

"I always sleep well. The trouble starts when you wake up." Gabriel got to his feet and stretched, working some of the kinks out of his muscles. He would have helped Cierra and Mariella up as well, but neither of them seemed interested in his help. They were too busy glaring at each other and at him.

"Any sign of Esparza and his men?" Gabriel asked as he went over to join Escalante and Tomás.

Escalante shook his head. "I thought I heard the sound of his trucks far in the distance a while ago, but I could not be sure."

"If he's still in the trucks, he won't be able to go much farther in them," Mariella said. "The trail isn't wide enough for them, and then there's the Blade of the Gods to consider."

"What's that?" Gabriel asked.

"A gorge that borders the valley on the west. It's narrow and very deep, as if someone had drawn a giant knife through the earth. On the eastern side of the valley, the mountains are impassable. Those two barriers are why Cuchatlán is so isolated, and why it has remained so for all these years."

"How do you get across this gorge?"

"There is a rope bridge. It will support men and even pack animals, but not trucks."

Gabriel nodded. This was a primitive land where they were going, but not a primitive people, he reminded himself. They knew quite a bit about the outside world in Cuchatlán, enough so that Mariella had been able to travel to New York City and function just fine. The gown she had worn that night at the Met, while presumably hand-sewn, could have passed for the height of current style. Hell, it *had* passed.

"What about between here and there?"

"There are several trails. I can guess which ones Hector is likely to show Esparza. We will take a different path, one that is shorter. And we can move faster, since our group is smaller."

Gabriel nodded. "We'd better get started. We don't want to blow whatever advantage we've got."

They made a quick breakfast on the provisions that had been left in the cave, then set out. Mariella led them along the ledge as it twisted downward, and soon they were back in the thick, junglelike forest. She took Escalante's machete and used it to chop away the vines that clogged the narrow path. This was some sort of game trail, Gabriel thought, and it took a considerable amount of work to widen it enough for them to use it. Mariella's fatigue shirt was dark with sweat and torn in several places by thorns that had caught it, but when he offered to spell her with the machete, she shook her head.

"No offense, Señor Hunt, but you would soon lose the path. I know where I'm going."

Unlike the cool, clear air where they had spent the night on the side of the mountain, down here the atmosphere was thick and muggy, and mosquitoes and other insects buzzed and whined around their heads. Once Mariella held up her hand in a signal for the others to stop, and they stood there silent and motionless as a snake twenty feet long and as big around as a man's leg slithered across the trail in front of them. Another time Mariella halted the group with the whispered warning, *"Tigre!"* and they waited nervously, listening to the nearby rustling in the brush, until the jaguar moved on.

All five of them were drenched in sweat by the time they trekked through another pass and then climbed down a steep slope, clinging to vines to keep their balance as they did so. "The Blade of the Gods is not far now," Mariella said as they paused to rest for a moment. "We will be in Cuchatlán in less than an hour."

That couldn't come soon enough to satisfy Gabriel, and the others were showing signs of impatience as well.

The jungle remained nearly impenetrable, right up to the point where it suddenly thinned out and they stepped onto a grassy verge about ten yards wide. After that, the ground dropped away into the yawning nothingness of the chasm Mariella had spoken of. The Blade of the Gods was a good name for it. Fifty yards wide, evidently hundreds of feet deep, its sides were perfectly sheer and dropped straight down. The chasm ran perfectly straight as well, due north and south as far as Gabriel could tell. It vanished in both directions, extending farther than the eye could see.

Mariella's knowledge and instincts had led them unerringly to the only spot where they could cross the chasm. A four-foot-wide bridge made of thick ropes and rough-hewn planks extended across the giant slash in the earth. Cierra muttered, *"Dios mio,"* when she saw it, and when Gabriel glanced over at her he saw the fear in her eyes. Even Escalante and Tomás, hardened though they were, looked a little nervous at the prospect of crossing that sagging span. A breeze drifted along the gorge and, at its touch, the bridge swayed back and forth.

"It's not as bad as it looks," Mariella said. "I've crossed it many times. Many of us who live in Cuchatlán have." She gave Cierra a slightly superior look. "If you're worried about it, I'll go first, so you can see how it's done."

"That's not necessary," Cierra replied with a defiant toss of her head, though her eyes still showed her ambivalence. "But will it hold all five of us?"

Mariella gestured toward the ropes that were attached to the sturdy pair of posts anchoring each end of the bridge. Those ropes were each as thick as a man's wrist. "The bridge will support all of us without any problem. I've seen fully loaded pack mules go across it."

"Let's go, then," Gabriel said. He was ready to see this so-called lost city of the Mayas for himself, and wanted to have as much time there before Esparza showed up as possible.

Mariella stepped out onto the bridge. The planks had gaps of several inches between them. She moved carefully but confidently, holding the machete in her left hand and the bridge's guide rope with her right. There was no guide rope on the left, only open air.

The bridge sagged even more under her weight. Gabriel saw the ropes attached to the anchor posts tighten around the wood.

"I'll go next," he said. "Cierra, you follow me." Escalante and Tomás could bring up the rear, Gabriel didn't care in which order.

Despite his generally steady nerves, he felt a tightening in his belly as he stepped out onto the span. The gaps between the planks gave him a very good view of the hundreds of feet of empty air underneath him. The gorge was a good four hundred feet deep. At the bottom of it ran a stream that appeared to be nothing more than a thread of silver from this height.

Mariella was four planks ahead of him. She glanced back over her shoulder and called, "Are you doing all right?"

"Fine," Gabriel replied. "No problem." He moved to the next plank and paused to look back at Cierra. "Come on. It'll be fine. Just hang on tight to the guide rope and don't look down."

Cierra swallowed hard and said, "I think you can count on that, Gabriel." She moved onto the first plank. She'd reached out and grasped the rope with her right hand before she stepped onto the rough board. It was clear that heights bothered her a great deal. Still, determination was etched on her face as well as fear. She stepped out with her left foot, rested it solidly on the next plank, and moved her right foot to join it.

Slowly, they worked their way out onto the bridge. Escalante and Tomás followed Cierra. Soon, all five of them were above the deep gorge. The ropes had sagged so much that their heads were below the level of the cliff on the far side.

This would be a heck of a place for a trap, Gabriel thought.

As if reading his thoughts, Mariella turned to look back at Gabriel and smiled in encouragement.

That smile disappeared abruptly, to be replaced by a look of shock and horror. Gabriel jerked his head around, knowing that Mariella had seen something behind them.

Alexei Podnemovitch had stepped out of the jungle at the western end of the bridge. He no longer wore the sling for his injured arm and shoulder but had a gun in that hand instead. Podnemovitch leveled the revolver at Gabriel and the others and said, "Not another step, Hunt."

Chapter 20

Looked like Mariella wasn't the only one who knew some hidden trails and shortcuts.

"What do you want, Podnemovitch?"

The big, broken-nosed man laughed. "What do I want? I want you dead, of course. Why don't you just go ahead and jump off that bridge? Save us all a lot of trouble, don't you think?"

"You first," Gabriel said between gritted teeth.

A couple of other men stepped out of the jungle behind Podnemovitch. One of them carried a rifle, and Gabriel assumed that he was one of Esparza's men. The other was short and slender and pale and wore a dirty, rumpled suit with no tie. He walked with a limp and used a branch in one hand for support. He laughed harshly and said, "You thought you could get here before me, didn't you, Mariella? Think you're so high and mighty, like you're the queen of Cuchatlán!"

"Hector!" she said. "You . . . you traitor!"

Hector gave a mockery of a salute. "Soon *I* will be the ruler of Cuchatlán! Señor Esparza has promised me that I will be in charge here!"

What a fool, thought Gabriel. No one, no matter how

self-deluded, should have been stupid enough to believe that promise, if indeed it had been made at all. The greed that had led Hector to betray his people in the first place was now blinding him to the truth of his own situation. He'd already been beaten to within an inch of his life, and as soon as Esparza had everything he wanted, that last inch would be taken from him as well.

But that time hadn't come yet. Which meant Esparza didn't have everything he wanted.

Podnemovitch said, "Step aside, Hunt, and let Señora Fargo past. Vladimir has decided that he will spare her life, as well as that of Dr. Almanzar. You and those two bandits, though, are of no worth to him." He used the revolver to gesture at Escalante and Tomás. "You two, out of the way! Let the women come back off the bridge."

"Gabriel," Cierra said, "as soon as we get off the bridge, that bastard will shoot you all."

In a low voice, he said, "When things start to happen, get around me, then you and Mariella make a run for the far side of the bridge."

"You mean abandon you?"

"I mean get out of the way so we can make a fight of it." Gabriel had heard voices not far away and knew that more men were coming. Esparza must have sent a few men hurrying ahead, but now the main party was approaching the Blade of the Gods. If Gabriel and his companions could just get across somehow and cut the ropes supporting the bridge before any of Esparza's men could cross . . .

Of course, that would trap them in the valley, he realized, but they could deal with that problem later, once they'd made sure that Esparza couldn't reach Cuchatlán.

"I'm losing patience, Hunt," Podnemovitch called. "Let the women off the bridge now."

Tomás took matters into his own hands then. The short bandit let out a yell of rage and hurled his machete end-over-end at Podnemovitch.

Gabriel brought up his Colt and yelled, "Go!" at Cierra.

Podnemovitch flung himself to the side and fired at Tomás, but the shot missed. At the same time Tomás charged toward the big Russian, bellowing in anger as he leaped from plank to plank, skipping every other one and causing the bridge to shake beneath him.

Cierra hurried toward Gabriel, who crowded against the guide rope to give her room to pass him. He reached out with his free hand to steady her, since she wouldn't have anything to hold on to.

She didn't get there, though. One of her feet slipped, and with a terrified cry her leg plunged between the planks. She started to tilt out to the side.

In desperation, Gabriel reached for her, caught hold of her shirt. It ripped down the front, the fabric parting under Cierra's weight. But the shirt didn't tear completely, and he was able to stop her fall and pull her halfway onto the bridge, which was now swaying worse than before.

Gabriel glanced up as shots roared out. He saw that Tomás had almost reached the end of the bridge, but Podnemovitch had set himself now and he didn't miss as flame spurted from the muzzle of the big revolver. Tomás jerked and slowed as the slugs plowed into his broad chest. His momentum kept him going all the way off the bridge, however, and he crashed into Podnemovitch.

The other man opened fire with his rifle. Gabriel and Escalante ducked as bullets whistled past them. Escalante brought his Springfield to his shoulder and squeezed off a round. Esparza's man doubled over as the bullet hit him in the midsection.

But his last shot had found a target, too, as Escalante twisted under its impact. Gabriel was trying to pull Cierra back fully onto the bridge—her leg still dangled through the gap between planks—as he saw Escalante fall perilously close to the edge. The bandit leader dropped his rifle. It slid off the bridge and fell, turning over and over in the air as it plummeted toward the stream far below.

Escalante went halfway off the bridge before he was able to grab hold of a plank. He pressed his other hand to the wound in his side. Blood pumped between his fingers.

"Hang on!" Gabriel shouted to him.

He struggled to lift Cierra, whose leg was now twisted and caught between the planks. A few feet away Escalante's fingers scrabbled at the wood as his legs dangled off the side of the bridge.

Somewhere behind Gabriel, Mariella screamed.

He jerked his head around to see that two more of Esparza's men had emerged from the thick growth at the *eastern* end of the bridge—the Cuchatlán side—and charged out onto the span. One of them had hold of Mariella and was trying to drag her off the bridge. The other came at Gabriel, his lips curled in a snarl.

Gabriel understood now what had happened. Hector had known a shortcut of his own and gotten a small group of Esparza's men to the gorge ahead of Gabriel and his companions. These men crossed the bridge to the eastern side and concealed themselves there. It had been a trap, all right, and Gabriel had walked into it.

With a desperate heave, he finally lifted Cierra onto the bridge. "Grab the rope and hang on," he told her. Then he swung around to face the man who was almost on top of him.

Gabriel hadn't had a chance to use his Colt yet, and he

didn't get that chance now. The man's hand chopped down in a vicious blow. The side of it caught Gabriel's wrist and knocked the gun loose. The Colt fell and landed on the planks at Gabriel's feet.

He didn't have time to try to retrieve it. Instead he swung a fist at the man's head, knocking him backward. As the bridge swayed to the side and the man almost pitched off of it into nothingness, he flung out a hand in desperation and grabbed the guide rope. He swung his foot up in a kick that landed in Gabriel's stomach and knocked him back against Cierra, who screamed again as she hung on to the guide rope for dear life. Her torn shirt hung open, her breasts barely covered beneath it in a red bra. The sight caught the eye of Esparza's man; he only hesitated a split second, but it was enough for Gabriel to bring his right fist up in a sizzling uppercut that landed solidly on the man's jaw.

This time the man didn't have a chance to grab the guide rope. The punch propelled him back and to the side, and suddenly there was nothing under him but air. He shrieked in terror as he fell, tumbling for a few seconds before he reached the bottom of the gorge and the fading screams abruptly stopped.

Gabriel glanced one way, saw that the second man had succeeded in dragging Mariella off the bridge. He looked the other way and saw Cierra still clinging to the guide rope. Escalante had finally been able to pull himself back onto the bridge, but he was still bleeding as he lay on the planks, breathing heavily.

At the western end of the bridge, Podnemovitch had gotten up after being knocked down by Tomás, who still lay there on the grassy verge. With his already ugly face made even uglier by the rage contorting his features, Podnemovitch stood over Tomás and pumped three more rounds into him, the shots slamming out and echoing back from the walls of the gorge.

Gabriel's Colt still lay on one of the rough-hewn planks, its muzzle lodged against a large splinter. That was all that had kept it from falling off while the bridge was swaying beneath them. Escalante reached out with a blood-covered hand and closed his fingers around the revolver's grip. He lifted it and fired at Podnemovitch, who ducked back toward the jungle. Over the echoing roar of the gun, Escalante shouted to Gabriel, "Take Cierra and go! I'll hold him here!"

Even if the bandit hadn't been wounded, Gabriel didn't think he would have been any match for the big Russian. He knew that Escalante was offering himself up as a sacrifice.

But that was Escalante's decision to make. He knew how badly he was hurt, knew he probably wouldn't make it anyway. Gabriel couldn't let that gesture go to waste, so he grabbed Cierra's arm and urged her toward the eastern end of the bridge.

"No!" she cried. "Paco!"

"Go!" Escalante told her.

Cierra sobbed as Gabriel dragged her toward the end of the bridge. There would still be Esparza's other man to deal with once they got there, but for now the important thing was to get off this perilous span.

As they approached the end of the bridge Gabriel saw that Mariella was still struggling with her captor. She landed a roundhouse punch as Gabriel and Cierra stumbled off the bridge. Solid ground had seldom felt as good under Gabriel's feet as it did at that moment.

As Cierra slumped to her knees, he let go of her arm and lunged forward to grab the shoulder of the man Mariella had just punched. The man was off balance from that blow, and Gabriel was able to jerk him around and throw a right cross that slammed into his jaw and put him down, out cold.

More shots blasted. Gabriel saw that Escalante had managed to pull himself to his feet. The bandit stood on the bridge shooting at Podnemovitch, who was returning the fire as he advanced, striding deliberately from plank to plank as he approached. Escalante's wound had weakened him to the point that his aim was shaky and his shots missed Podnemovitch.

Not so the slugs fired by the big Russian. They pounded into Escalante and slewed the bandit around. Escalante grabbed the rope with his free hand and looked back at Gabriel, Cierra, and Mariella.

"Cut the ropes!" he cried with fading strength. "Cut the ropes, Gabriel!"

Gabriel looked down at the man he had just knocked out, saw a sheathed machete at his waist. He bent and yanked the big blade from its sheath, spun toward the bridge. "Head for the jungle!" he told Cierra and Mariella as he slashed at the anchor ropes.

Podnemovitch roared something in Russian that sounded like a curse. He fired past the sagging Escalante at Gabriel, who brought the machete chopping down on the rope again. One of Podnemovitch's bullets chewed splinters from the anchor post. Gabriel thought one more strike might part the rope, which would cause the bridge to twist and throw Podnemovitch off into the gorge.

Before the machete could fall, though, Cierra and Mariella both cried out in alarm. A new voice called, "Drop the machete, Señor Hunt, or my men will kill you and the women both."

Gabriel recognized those arrogant tones. He looked behind him and saw that Vladimir Antonio de la Esparza had emerged from the jungle on *this* side of the bridge, along with a dozen heavily armed men who had rifles trained on him.

So much for a small group having reached the bridge before them. *All* of them had made it here and crossed over the gorge, leaving only Podnemovitch and a few other men to follow behind and set up the ambush.

He wasn't ready to drop the machete just yet, though. He said, "Back off, Esparza. You can't have me gunned down fast enough to stop me from cutting this rope, and if I do, Podnemovitch better know how to fly."

The threat didn't appear to ruffle Esparza. "If you do that, Señor Hunt," he said as he brought up a pistol and pointed it at Cierra, "I will kill Dr. Almanzar and then have my men shoot you."

"Do it, Gabriel!" Cierra cried. "I don't care what happens to me! Just do it!"

Gabriel glanced along the bridge at Podnemovitch, who now stood over Escalante's motionless body with a tensely expectant look on his face. He had to know that he didn't have time to make it back to the other end of the bridge before Gabriel could chop through the final strands of the rope.

But Gabriel couldn't do it. Slowly, he lowered the machete, then let the handle slip through his fingers. The big knife fell to the ground at his feet.

"Very wise, Señor Hunt," Esparza said. "More wise than you know. You see, I've decided that I'm going to let you live for the time being. I want you to witness my triumphant entry into Cuchatlán."

Gabriel didn't say anything. Cursing wouldn't help matters.

He looked back out onto the bridge and saw Podnemovitch reach down to pick up the Colt Escalante had dropped. As Podnemovitch did so, Escalante's hand came up and caught feebly at his arm, as if the bandit were trying to throw him off the bridge. That surprised Gabriel a little, since he had thought that Escalante was already dead.

Escalante was too weak to budge Podnemovitch. The Russian laughed harshly, straightened, and said, "Old fool." He hooked a toe under Escalante's shoulder and rolled him off the bridge. Cierra screamed in horror as Escalante fell, but not a sound came from the bandit himself.

Gabriel looked away, not wanting to see the end of Escalante's plunge into the gorge. He saw that Mariella had put her arms around Cierra and turned her away from the chasm as well. Whatever friction there had been between the two women was gone; they had worse enemies to face than each other now.

"Bring all three of the prisoners," Esparza snapped at his men.

Podnemovitch reached the eastern end of the bridge. The traitor Hector limped across after him. Podnemovitch said, "When the time comes for Hunt to die, Vladimir, I want to be the one to kill him."

"Of course, Alexei," Esparza replied with a smile. "I think you've earned that right. Señor Hunt has proven hard to kill, though." His voice hardened slightly. "Next time, make certain that he's dead."

With that he turned to stalk onto a trail through the jungle, and his men surrounded Gabriel, Cierra, and Mariella and prodded them along after him.

Gabriel thought bitterly about the turn events had taken. He would soon see the ruins of Cuchatlán for himself . . . but not the way he had intended.

Chapter 21

The valley was beautiful, no doubt about that, Gabriel thought as the group topped a small rise that gave them a good view of the land spread out before them. Lush and green, stretching for miles between the gorge known as the Blade of the Gods on the west and a wall-like range of cloud-wreathed mountains to the east, the valley gave every appearance of being, as Mariella had said, paradise.

What looked, at first glance, like several small hills rose from the valley floor about a mile away. Gabriel looked closer and realized that instead of hills, they were Mayan pyramids that were so covered with the vines that had grown over the centuries they looked like natural formations rather than man-made structures. A shorter, squatly built hump near the pyramids was probably some sort of ancient palace.

"I don't believe it," Cierra said as she trudged along beside Gabriel. "Why has this place never been discovered before now?"

"Think about how inaccessible it is," Gabriel said. "If you came up to that gorge and didn't know there was a bridge over it, you might just turn back. And Mariella said there are no passes through those mountains to the east, so nobody could get in that way."

"Yes, but it should have been spotted from the air," Cierra insisted. "That's the way some of the other lost Mayan cities have been found, by people searching with planes and helicopters."

"Again, the mountains probably have something to do with it. They're high enough so that an approach from that direction wouldn't be easy. Not impossible, mind you, but not easy, either. And even if somebody flew over the valley, what would they see? Some hills?"

Mariella was walking in front of them, flanked by two of Esparza's men. Esparza was up ahead, striding along with Podnemovitch beside him. Mariella turned to look at Gabriel and Cierra, and it was obvious she had been listening to their conversation as she said, "Cuchatlán was abandoned by the Maya earlier than any of their other cities. The vegetation has had more time to cover the old ruins. That's why they're so well hidden. You would have to know it was there, like Granville did, to have much of a chance of finding it."

"You still insist that fantastic story about the Well of Eternity is true?" Cierra wanted to know.

"Of course it's true. Would so many people have died because of it if it was only a legend?"

Gabriel refrained from reminding her how full history was of men dying because of legends.

Mariella stumbled a bit as she turned toward the front of the group again, caught herself, and passed a hand wearily over her face. Gabriel thought she looked more fatigued, more haggard, than she had earlier.

Almost like she was starting to show those more than one hundred fifty years she claimed to possess.

Gabriel moved up beside Mariella. Esparza's men

watched him closely but didn't try to stop him. "Who exactly lives here now?" he asked. "You said the Maya abandoned the city when they began moving northward into Chiapas and the Yucatan."

She nodded. "Other Indians in the region moved in once the Maya were gone. When Granville and his men—and I—reached Cuchatlán . . . I think it was in 1866, though of course it was hard to keep track of dates here in the jungle . . . the Indians who had established a village near the ruins welcomed us. They shared the waters of the Well with us, though we didn't understand yet what they could do. Granville's men liked it here, and so did I. We persuaded him to stay for a time, to let the men rest. He'd been talking about taking samples of the water overseas, offering it to Queen Victoria if Great Britain would throw all its power and influence behind a new Confederacy." Mariella smiled. "But he'd been talking about it less and less as time went on, and he talked about it less still once we were here. Finally the beauty of this place seduced Granville, just as it did the rest of us. He has never left. His men married into the tribe. Over the decades we have all become one people, the people of Cuchatlán."

"Wait a minute," Cierra said. "If this is true, if all of you who live in this valley are well over a hundred years old, the population should have increased exponentially until there were thousands and thousands of you . . . perhaps hundreds of thousands."

Mariella shook her head. "The waters of the Well do not confer invulnerability, just immunity to aging. It's true that they allow us to recover quickly from illness or injury, but if someone is hurt badly enough, he dies. Accidents happen. People are crushed by snakes or mauled by jaguars. They have falls. Such things keep the population down." A sad smile came over her tired face. "And truly, everything comes with a price. People who drink from the Well of Eternity . . . have very few children."

"It causes sterility," Gabriel said.

"Not in everyone. But the women of the valley have a hard time getting with child. And when they do, the pregnancies are difficult. The babies often do not survive."

"It sounds like something in the water causes genetic mutations," Cierra muttered reluctantly, realizing, Gabriel figured, that this admission on her part was tantamount to an admission that everything Mariella had told them might be true.

"The gods give with one hand and take away with the other," Mariella said.

Esparza looked back at them. He had evidently been listening, too. "Once my scientists have analyzed the water and unlocked its secrets, something will be done about the side effects. The water will be perfected by the time I am ready to share it with the world."

"You mean sell it to the world, don't you?" Gabriel asked.

"Anyone who brings such a boon to mankind as eternal life deserves to be rewarded, don't you think?" Esparza chuckled. "And with more than mere wealth. How does . . . emperor sound to you?"

"Of Cuchatlán?"

"Of the world, Mr. Hunt."

"It sounds like the ravings of a madman," Gabriel said.

Esparza's mouth tightened into an angry line, but he didn't say anything else to the prisoners. Instead he turned to Podnemovitch and ordered, "When we get there, have them taken to the palace with the others."

"The others?" Mariella repeated. "My husband! Where is my husband?"

"Don't worry about General Fargo," Esparza said. "He's alive, merely a prisoner now, like the rest."

Gabriel wondered how Esparza had managed to conquer the whole valley with only a handful of men, but he got the answer to that question a few minutes later when they entered the village and he saw the machine guns. Previously mounted on the trucks, they had been taken loose from their mounts, hauled all the way here, and set up to rake the village's wooden huts with deadly .50-caliber fire. Several of the huts had been shot practically to pieces. General Fargo must have ordered his men to surrender rather than have all the people of Cuchatlán slaughtered.

"Didn't you have any modern weapons to defend yourselves?" Gabriel asked Mariella in an undertone. "Your people must have some money if they travel out of the valley from time to time, like you said. You could have bought some."

"Granville gave up war when he decided not to leave the valley," she said. "He said the weapons his men had were enough to protect us from wild animals and for hunting. He said he had had enough of killing."

That was an admirable attitude, thought Gabriel . . . but only if everybody else you were likely to encounter shared it. If they didn't, then sooner or later you were in for a lot of trouble. As General Fargo had discovered today.

Though it had worked for him for a long time. Gabriel had to admit that much. Fargo had had almost a hundred and fifty years in these idyllic surroundings, with a beautiful, intelligent woman at his side. That was way more than any normal man could hope for.

The three pyramids formed a rough triangle, with the

palace sitting along one leg of the triangle between two of them. In the center of the triangle was a broad, round plaza made of intricately interlocking flat stones. The stones had been painted subtly differing shades of green and brown and tan, so that from the air they would look like a clearing in the jungle, but not necessarily a manmade one. A large, flat, circular stone sat in the middle of the plaza. It was probably ten feet in diameter, a couple of feet thick, and must have weighed at least a thousand pounds. It wasn't so heavy that it couldn't be moved if enough men were pushing it, though. That was obvious from the markings on the flagstones where it had been shoved aside.

The circular stone was a well cover, Gabriel realized as he saw the four-foot-wide hole that had been revealed when the rock was moved. "The Well of Eternity," Esparza said in a voice that betrayed a touch of awe as he came to a stop beside it.

"The Maya used to sacrifice virgins by throwing them in wells like that," Cierra said. "They were considered entrances to the realm of the gods."

Esparza smiled at her. "Don't worry, my dear. Such a fate won't befall you. As I'm sure Mr. Hunt can attest, you would hardly qualify anyway."

Cierra's eyes narrowed angrily, but she didn't say anything else. Esparza motioned to his men, and the prisoners were prodded on toward the palace.

Although it was a lot shorter than the nearby pyramids, no more than thirty or forty feet tall rather than a hundred feet or more, its base shared the same sort of construction. A series of terraced steps, only rising to a long, columned building instead of continuing on up to tiny temples.

For no particularly good reason other than raw curiosity, Gabriel counted the steps as they were marched up to the palace. There were thirty of them, each a little more than a foot tall. When they reached the top, they were herded through an arched entrance into a room with more steps, these leading down.

"See that they're locked up," Esparza told Podnemovitch. "I'll decide what to do with them later." He smiled at Mariella. "We might as well allow Señora Fargo to be reunited with her husband for a short time. We are not brutes, after all."

Podnemovitch and his men marched the three prisoners down the stone stairs, which were lit by occasional candles guttering in niches set into the walls. The walls were made of large blocks of stone, and as the group went deeper, beads of moisture began to appear on the walls, trickling down them. Gabriel estimated that they had descended far enough to be underground now, and the dampness confirmed that guess.

The stairs finally came to a stop in front of a door that was nothing more than a single massive slab of stone. Several of Esparza's men occupied the space in front of the door. They were holding automatic weapons.

Podnemovitch motioned for the guards to step back. The big Russian pushed a small lever that protruded from the wall, and with a grating sound the door began to move inward in a slow, ponderous swinging motion. It was a good two feet thick.

"A counterweight and balance mechanism," Cierra said under her breath. "Fascinating."

Gabriel found it interesting himself, though it wasn't the first time he'd seen such a mechanism. Ancient architects in vanished civilizations all over the world had been capable of some amazing things, despite the rather primitive tools with which they had to work. They had some surprising holes in their knowledge, though, he thought, recalling that the Maya, for example, had never mastered the concept of the wheel. If they had, there was no way of knowing how far their empire might have extended.

"Inside," Podnemovitch ordered. Heavily outnumbered and under the gun, the prisoners had no choice but to obey. Gabriel, Cierra, and Mariella moved into the vast, open space on the other side of the door. Sunlight filtered down through occasional cracks in the ceiling and it was just bright enough for Gabriel to be able to make out shadowy figures spread around the room. As the door scraped shut, those figures began to converge on the newcomers. Gabriel felt a shiver go through him. They were like phantoms flocking around newly lost souls who had just arrived in purgatory.

That sensation went away, though, as the other prisoners came closer and he saw that they were just men and women like himself . . . well, just like him other than the fact that some of them might be hundreds of years old.

And some of them looked it, too. Many of the faces peering at him were lined and cracked by the ravages of time. He wondered what the hell was going on here. Wasn't the Well of Eternity supposed to keep these people young and vital?

"Mariella!" a husky voice rasped. "My God, is it really you?"

The crowd of prisoners parted to let a tall man through. As he stepped forward, Mariella cried, "Granville!" and rushed into his arms.

He held her tightly and trembled with emotion. "That . . that scoundrel who calls himself Esparza said that you would soon be his captive, but I was praying that it wasn't so! Oh, my dear, I wish you had never come back to Cuchatlán."

"I would have come back no matter what," she whispered. "I could never be away from you for long, my love."

The man kissed her, hugged her, stroked her hair. Then he looked past her shoulder at the other newcomers and asked in a voice that still held a soft Southern drawl, "Who are these people?"

Gabriel hadn't gotten a good look at the man yet, but as Mariella turned and led him forward into one of the slender shafts of light, Gabriel saw him clearly. The man was tall and lean, with deep-set eyes and a closely trimmed beard. The beard was completely white, as was the shock of hair on his head. Deep trenches were etched in his cheeks. He looked a lot older than he had in the picture Gabriel had seen in the book at Olustee, but that made sense considering that this man was probably more than a hundred and seventy years old. Gabriel's heart thudded hard in his chest as that realization sunk in. He didn't doubt Mariella's story anymore, not at all.

"Gabriel Hunt," Mariella said, "I would like for you to meet my husband, General Granville Fordham Fargo."

Chapter 22

The general extended his hand. "Mr. Hunt," he said. "I'm very pleased to meet you, sir, although I wish it had been under better circumstances."

"So do I, General," Gabriel said as he gripped Fargo's hand.

"Excuse me," Cierra said. "You're really . . . General Fargo . . . from the U.S. Civil War?"

A gentle smile appeared on Fargo's weathered face. "That was a long time ago, my dear. I'd like to think I'll be remembered more for what I've done in the fourteen decades since. But yes—I am that man, and yes, I once fought that war. And you are . . . ?"

"Dr. Cierra Almanzar. Director of the Museum of the Americas in Mexico City."

Fargo took her hand, and for a second Gabriel thought he was going to bend over it and kiss it. Most Confederate cavalry officers had fancied themselves cavaliers in the old-fashioned sense of the word, he recalled reading, and that would be a very cavalier-like thing to do.

Instead, Fargo merely shook Cierra's hand and said, "I'm very pleased to meet you as well, Dr. Almanzar. I have heard of you. I believe your museum houses one of my battle flags, the one I left with my father-in-law."

"It used to," Gabriel said. "Not anymore." He began unbuttoning his shirt. "I have it here, along with the one you drew the map on."

"My standard?" Fargo murmured in surprise. "You brought it with you? I was hoping that your brother had it by now, along with the sample of water I sent with Mariella."

"The sample was . . . destroyed, Granville." Mariella's voice caught a little as she broke the news to him. "It was lost before I ever got the chance to tell Señor Hunt about it."

Gabriel stopped unbuttoning his shirt. After the news that Mariella had just broken to the general, the flags didn't seem so important anymore.

A pained look appeared on Fargo's face. He expelled a long, disappointed breath.

"I'm dismayed to hear that. Not so much for myself, but for all my friends and loved ones here in Cuchatlán who are now doomed."

"Doomed?" Mariella repeated as she clutched at her husband's arm. "Granville, what are you talking about?"

Fargo turned to her and rested his hands on her shoulders. "I didn't tell you the full extent of your errand, dearest. My hope was that Michael Hunt and the scientists he could hire would be able to find out what gives the waters of the Well their special power."

"I know that," Mariella said with a nod. "You told me to tell Señor Hunt that he should have the water analyzed and find out everything that's in it."

"But I didn't tell you why. It wasn't simply in the hope that the water's special ingredients could somehow be duplicated. It was because the water here . . . the water from the Well . . ."

Fargo couldn't bring himself to go on. He looked stricken now, and his hands tightened on Mariella's shoulders.

Gabriel finished the sentence for the general as everything fell into place. "The water from the Well of Eternity is losing its power," he said.

Fargo turned to look at him and slowly nodded. "I'm afraid that is correct, Mr. Hunt. I first noticed a few years ago among the older citizens of Cuchatlán. After the Ritual of the Well, they didn't recover their vitality as quickly as they used to. Their muscles regained less elasticity. Their skin remained lined, their energy depleted. I felt it myself."

"Granville, no," Mariella cried. "The water of the Well still works—it must! It always has!"

Fargo shook his head. "Look around you, my dear. Look inside yourself." He turned to Gabriel and Cierra. "The last ritual was a month ago, not long before I sent Mariella to you. I knew then that time was short, because I could tell that there was only a small effect when our people drank from the Well. Its power is almost gone. If there was to be any chance of ever fathoming its secrets, I had to act."

Mariella put her arms around him and buried her face against his chest. "You should have told me," she said, her voice muffled by the embrace. "If our time was running out, we should have spent all of it we had left together."

"I wanted to," Fargo told her. "You don't know how badly I wanted to. But I thought . . . if there was still a chance of helping our people . . ."

Mariella nodded her head against his chest. "I understand. You've always looked out for those who followed you."

"It's ironic," Gabriel said. "Esparza has come all this way, wreaked so much havoc and killed so many people, and what he's after doesn't even work anymore."

Fargo stroked the back of his wife's head. "It would have been worth the greatest fortune in the world at one time. But no longer."

"Wait a minute," Cierra said. "Let's think about this. Assuming the water ever had any power, the fact that its power has diminished wouldn't mean there's nothing of value here at all. You could still analyze it, figure out what produces the life-extending effect. Once the cause were isolated, a well-equipped lab working on the problem might be able to find a way to enhance its activity. And even if they couldn't, if the water still has any effect at all . . . wouldn't men still kill for even a less potent elixir?"

"Why, Cierra," Gabriel said, "you sound like a believer suddenly."

"I am a scientist. I believe in evidence. The only other explanation for what we see here is that all these people are delusional and suffering from mass hysteria."

"We're quite sane, doctor, I assure you," Fargo said with a sad smile.

"Well, then, the power of the water must come from somewhere, from something. Some mineral deposit buried deep in the mountains, something the water passes through or over before it emerges here. Over enough centuries, even the most massive mineral deposit will eventually be eroded to nothing. That's one hypothesis that might account for the diminished potency. In that case it wouldn't be the water itself that has the life-extending effect, it's whatever the water picks up as it flows underground. And if we could learn what that is—"

"That's what I hoped the Hunt Foundation could do," Fargo said to Gabriel

"That's Michael's area, not mine," Gabriel said. "He's no chemist himself, for that matter. But he's got access to some of the finest minds in the world."

Fargo nodded. "I wanted to get those men to work on our problem. Not necessarily to save all of *us*, mind you, because I fear it's too late for that. But for the sake of all the good it could do in the world. And if I could at least save Mariella, well . . ."

She shook her head. "You old fool," she said softly. "Do you think I would want to live without you? It was only being with you that made all these years worthwhile in the first place."

Fargo sighed. "No matter. Now it's too late for us all. Those . . . those barbarians with their Gatling guns—" He waved a hand. "I know, they're not Gatling guns. They're something even worse. I never wanted the artifacts of warfare to pollute this valley."

"That's an unusual attitude for a man who was a warrior," Gabriel pointed out.

"That was a very short period in a very long life, Mr. Hunt. I was a professor first. And when I got here, I discovered more than just this—I discovered that I'd had my fill of war. I couldn't stomach it anymore. And I came to understand that some of the things I'd fought for . . . just weren't worth fighting for." Fargo held out his hand. "Can I see those flags you brought with you?"

Gabriel untied the strips that held the folded flags to his torso. "I'm afraid they have more blood and sweat on them than they started out with," he said as he handed them to the general.

"A good man's blood and sweat are worthy stains, sir," Fargo said.

A couple of men stepped forward from the crowd of other prisoners. "Gen'ral?" one of them said. "The fellas would sure admire to see those colors again."

"Of course, Boone," Fargo replied. He handed the flags to the men, who unfolded them and held them up for the other prisoners to see. The men of the Fifth Georgia looked on them with silent reverence.

"I hate to tell you, General, but a hundred forty years later, those flags aren't exactly a popular sight where I come from," Gabriel said.

"They weren't always popular even back then, Mr. Hunt," Fargo said. "We lost the war, I'll remind you. But my men still rode below those colors. Don't begrudge them a moment of remembrance."

"They can have all the moments they want," Gabriel said. "At least till Esparza comes back."

"I wish," Fargo said after a moment, and then paused. "I almost wish . . ." His voice choked, he couldn't go on. But Gabriel got the gist of what he was trying to say.

"You wish that, if you have to go, you could go out fighting?"

"Now that we have something that really is worth fighting for? More than you know, Mr. Hunt. More than you can know."

"Well, why can't you? It's better than lying down and dying." Gabriel put an arm around the general's shoulders. "Let's see if we can figure something out."

"Hey!" Gabriel yelled as he put his mouth close to the crack at the edge of the door. "Hey, out there! Open up! I've got something your boss wants!"

"By God, sir!" General Fargo bellowed. "Give me back those flags!"

"Stand back," Gabriel shouted "or I'll break your

damn neck. Those flags are my ticket out of here. Guards! Tell Esparza I have the general's secret!"

"Damn your eyes," Fargo yelled, "I'll never let you do it!"

Gabriel heard the guards talking in low, urgent voices on the other side of the door and gave the general a silent thumbs-up. Fargo looked puzzled by the gesture and by the A-OK gesture Gabriel replaced it with. What gesture had they used back in Civil War days? Gabriel settled for nodding and this, at least, the general seemed to grasp.

"Back off in there!" one of the guards called a moment later. "We'll cut you all down if you try anything."

With a low rumble of stone against stone, the door began to swing inward.

Cierra had her ear pressed to the wall near one side of the door. She glanced at Gabriel and nodded, then stepped back away from the wall as the door opened the rest of the way. Gabriel and Fargo had backed away from it as well. Gabriel held both battle flags.

One guard came into the chamber while the other two remained outside, their automatic weapons leveled.

"What the hell do you want?" he demanded. "What was all the yelling about?"

Gabriel showed him the flags. "Take me to Señor Esparza," he said. "He'll want these."

One of the other guards said, "I remember Podnem'vitch saying something about flags. Maybe these are the ones."

"Give me those," the first guard snapped, reaching out for the flags.

Gabriel stepped back, but the other two guards pointed their guns at him. He stopped, grimaced, and then finally handed over the flags.

"All right. But you be sure and tell Esparza that I gave them to you. They're very important."

The flags meant nothing now, of course. But Esparza's men didn't know that.

"And tell him there's a hidden message on them. I can tell him how to read it."

"Don't do it, Hunt," Fargo growled. "You'll burn in hell for it." He was laying it on a bit thick, Gabriel thought, but the guards showed no signs of doubting his sincerity.

Holding the flags in one hand and his gun in the other, the guard backed out of the chamber. As soon as the closing door cut off his view, Cierra darted forward and pressed her ear to the stone again, this time at a spot a bit lower on the wall.

"Well?" Gabriel said, once the door was fully shut.

She hurried over to Gabriel and said in a low voice, "No question, the mechanism is on that side, about four feet up. The stone must be hollow there—I could hear the mechanism working. If we can get to it, we might be able to trip it from in here."

"And that would cause the door to open."

"It should, exactly the same as pushing the lever from outside."

Gabriel nodded. "The question now is whether or not we can loosen one of these blocks of stone enough to move it out."

He took off his belt and began using the buckle to scrape away at the layer of crude mortar between the blocks. The passing centuries had weakened the mortar and made it crumble easily, but even so this would be a long, tedious job.

At least, it would have been for one man. Several other prisoners gathered around, including Fargo and Boone.

They took off their belts and began scraping at the mortar as well.

As they worked, Boone said, "I heard you talkin' to Miz Fargo, Gen'ral. Is it true what you said, about the water not keepin' us young anymore?"

"I'm afraid so, Boone," Fargo said.

"I thought I'd been feelin' a mite puny lately. And Virginia, she's got a whole heap more gray in her hair than she did even a week ago. All those years are gonna catch up to us in a hurry, ain't they?"

"That looks to be the case."

"Well, hell." Boone shook his head. "Can't complain too much, I reckon, after all the years we cheated death outa'. When we rode away after Gen'ral Lee surrendered, I don't reckon any of us figured on livin' another hundred and fifty years in the prettiest place on God's green earth." The sergeant smiled ruefully. "With some of the prettiest gals, too."

"It's been a good sojourn, hasn't it?" Fargo said.

"It surely has, sir. It surely has."

They kept working. The beams of light slanting down into the prison chamber moved as the day wore on and finally began to wane. It would be easier to move around Cuchatlán without being spotted after dark, but Gabriel didn't know if Esparza would allow them that much time. Esparza didn't really need to keep any of them alive anymore, unless he believed that story about a hidden message on the flags.

By the time the direct sunlight had faded entirely, leaving them in a sepulchral twilight gloom, the men had gouged out enough mortar around the stone that they could get their fingers into the gap all around it. They began heaving on it, trying to work it back and forth. At first the remaining mortar resisted their efforts, but finally, with tiny grating sounds and even tinier movements, the stone began to shift.

With each movement of millimeters, the block loosened a little more. The men began to tug on it. It didn't want to budge, and for the longest time it didn't—but then gradually it began to come free. The men hauled it out slowly and, straining under the weight, set it carefully on the floor.

"The walls of these temples and palaces often have double layers," Cierra said, "with hollow spaces in between. That gives mechanisms like this one room to work."

Gabriel peered into the black opening where the stone block had been. His Zippo was still in one of the buttoned-up pockets of his shirt. He fished it out, hoping that it would work after its immersion in the Black River.

The lighter only sparked the first couple of times he spun the wheel, but then the flame caught. He held it inside the hole in the wall and studied what he could see of the mechanism from this side. He couldn't see where the lever attached to it.

"I'm going to have to crawl into this thing," he said.

Boone held the lighter while Gabriel wedged his head and shoulders into the opening. They barely fit. His shoulders scraped against the rough stone on either side as he edged forward. He reached one hand back between his legs and felt the Zippo deposited in it. He brought the lighter forward, saw the play of the orange flame on the stone all around him.

Now he could see into the space where the apparatus was located. The lever on the outside of the chamber raised a stone rod that set off the movement of counterweights attached to either side of a delicate metal chain.

Gabriel studied it until he had the whole setup committed to memory, then wriggled back out of the hole.

"We can do it," he reported to the others.

General Fargo jerked his head in a curt nod. His spine was straight, and there was an air of command about him that hadn't been there earlier. "Very well," he said. He turned to Boone. "Sergeant, get the women and children back in the far corner of the chamber."

"Not me," Mariella said. "I'm staying with you, Granville."

"I'm not going in any corner, either," Cierra added.

"You can argue with them if you want to, General," Gabriel said, "but you'd be wasting your time."

"Very well," Fargo said. "You two stay up here, but if there's any shooting I expect you to get down and stay down."

They didn't agree to that, but they didn't argue the point, either.

"When the door opens, the rest of you back off as well," Gabriel said. "We want to get at least two of the guards in here."

Fargo nodded. "Are you ready to proceed, Mr. Hunt?"

Gabriel looked around the room and saw that the shadows had thickened considerably. Not much light was left outside. The timing was good.

"Let's do it," he said.

Chapter 23

Now that he had familiarized himself with the mechanism, Gabriel didn't have to climb all the way back into the hole. He lit the Zippo again and set it down on the stone surface, then reached in with one arm extended. He was able to reach the end of the stone rod with his fingertips. He felt his fingers brush against the links of the metal chain, saw the shadows shift as the counterweights swung. With a glance first at Cierra, then Mariella, and then General Fargo, he gave a nod, then gently lifted the rod.

He felt the counterweights activate.

A rumbling sound came from within the wall as the mechanism began rotating the heavy door on its axis.

Gabriel heard the guards shouting as they noticed what was happening. "Stand back!" one of them yelled. "What are you doing in there?"

"We're not doing anything!" Fargo called back. "It just started opening on its own!"

The door was no longer flush with the wall on the inside of the chamber. Gabriel leaped up, caught hold of the upper edge of the door, and hung there as it continued its ponderous movement. When there was room, he pulled himself up, hooked a leg over the top of the door, and rolled onto it. The door was two feet thick and a good ten feet tall. If they had looked up, the guards might have been able to see Gabriel stretched out on top of it, but all their attention was focused on the other prisoners as they advanced into the chamber, brandishing their guns.

Of course, only two of the guards came in; the third stayed outside. It would have been best if all three had come in, but Gabriel hadn't expected that—professionals knew better.

The man still outside the door said, "I'm going to call Podnem'vitch on the radio and tell him something funny's going on here!"

Gabriel knew they couldn't let that happen. He pushed up onto his hands and knees and then dived off the door, landing on the two guards inside the chamber.

His arms went around their necks and slammed their heads together as the impact of his weight drove them forward. The satisfying crack of bone against bone told him that they wouldn't be waking up for a while.

But the third guard was still out there and had to be dealt with quickly. Before Gabriel could move, though, a big figure leaped over him and the two men he had knocked out. Boone crashed into the remaining guard just as the man jerked the trigger on his gun.

Boone's body muffled the automatic weapon's chatter. The sergeant's momentum bore the guard over backward. The man's head hit the edge of one of the stone steps with a crack, and the gun fell silent.

Boone rolled off the man. The burst of gunfire had ripped his midsection to pieces. His shirt was soaked with blood. He pressed his hands to his belly to hold in his ruined guts as one of the female prisoners rushed forward and threw herself on him, sobbing. That would be Virginia, Gabriel thought as he stood up.

Fargo moved to comfort the woman, Mariella coming after him. Boone's eyes flickered open. "Did I . . . get him, Gen'ral?"

"You certainly did, Sergeant," Fargo told him. "That was exemplary behavior. Exemplary, Seth."

"Thanks . . . Gen'ral." He glanced down at himself. "I reckon I could . . . drink up the whole well . . . and it wouldn't help me none . . . even if the water still worked . . . oh, Virginia . . ."

His wife threw her arms around him again as his final breath drained from his body.

Gabriel picked up the weapons Esparza's men had dropped. He handed one of them to Fargo, saying, "You know how to use one of these, General?"

"Looks to have a trigger," Fargo said. "I think I can figure it out."

Cierra stepped forward and held out her hand. "Give me one, Gabriel. I certainly know how to use it."

She certainly did. Gabriel handed over the weapon.

"Your men must have had *some* firearms—your old pistols or rifles, if nothing else," he said to Fargo. "Do you know what Esparza's men did with them after he forced you to surrender?"

One of Fargo's crew spoke up. "I saw them takin' the guns into the infirmary, General."

"They probably won't waste much effort guarding old weapons like that," Gabriel said. "Especially with the lot of you all safely locked up. But I'll bet you could do some damage with them if you got your hands on them again."

"Damned right we could," another man said. "That old muzzle-loader of mine is the sweetest rifle I ever held."

"Well, they make 'em sweeter today," Gabriel said, "but it'll have to do."

One of the women stepped forward. "I'll go with Matthew. The two of us, we'll get the guns."

"It'll take more than two," another woman said. "Count me in." And a man beside her stepped forward as well.

Was it bravery, or just that they had nothing to lose now that all the long years were about to come crashing down on them? A little of both, Gabriel thought. And did it matter more of which?

"Any of you that want to fight are welcome," he said. "Any that don't, that's fine, too. Just keep out of the way." He nodded toward the stairs that led up to the rest of the palace. "The general, Dr. Almanzar, and I will lead the way, since we're already armed. Join in when you can. Use any weapons you can find."

As they started up the steps, Cierra moved closer to Gabriel and took hold of his arm. "Against machine guns?" she whispered. "This is suicide. We're leading these people to their deaths."

"And ours?" Gabriel said. "Let's hope not."

When they reached the top of the stairs, Gabriel scouted the shadowy ground floor while the others waited. Voices led him to the terraced steps outside. Seven or eight of Esparza's men were sitting there smoking and passing a bottle back and forth.

Just past them he saw one of the machine guns. It had been lugged up the steps and set up in front of the palace entrance so that it covered the triangular area between the temple pyramids. If the people of Cuchatlán could get control of that gun, the odds against them would look a lot better . . .

Gabriel drifted back through the shadows to the others. He explained the situation to them. "If we can rush them and take them without a lot of commotion, we'll have that fifty caliber on our side and still have the element of surprise with us."

"I'll do it," Fargo said. He pointed to half a dozen men who swiftly assembled in a circle around him. The men armed themselves with makeshift bludgeons, chunks of broken rock they picked up from the floor as they went. Following close behind Fargo and Gabriel, darting from pillar to pillar, they approached the terraced steps and came up behind Esparza's men.

The moon was rising over the mountains now, flooding the valley with silvery light. Pausing just inside the arched entrance to the palace, Gabriel and Fargo looked at each other and exchanged a nod. Then Fargo raised an arm and swiftly swung it down, signaling his men to charge.

Gabriel and the general were in the lead as they rushed out. Esparza's men were talking and laughing among themselves, and they didn't hear the slap of hurrying feet on stone until it was too late. Gabriel swung the butt of the automatic weapon in his hand and crashed it into the back of a man's head. The others struck right behind him. Esparza's men fell under the unexpected attack, slumping to the steps one by one.

Now the prisoners had eight more automatic weapons—and the machine gun. Gabriel moved among the men, quickly demonstrating how to use the weapons. He picked out a couple of men to handle the machine gun. It would have been helpful if they could have practiced with the weapons before having to use them, but you couldn't ask for everything.

He found the man who had seen where the rifles had been taken and said, "Take some of the men and get to that infirmary. Arm yourselves and spread out, but stay out of sight until the shooting starts. Then pick off as many of Esparza's men as you can." He turned to the machine gunners. "You can see Esparza's camp over by that pyramid from here. When all hell breaks loose, hose it down good."

The men looked to Fargo for confirmation of the orders. The general nodded. "All of you do as Mr. Hunt says. I believe he has the makings of a good field officer."

Gabriel grinned. "I don't know about that. There are too many rules in the army for me."

"Only ever been one rule that counts in any army," Fargo said. "Win your battles."

Once the other group had stolen off into the shadows, Gabriel, Fargo, and the rest of the former prisoners made their way toward a ring of portable lights Esparza had set up around the Well.

"General Jackson was a master of splitting his forces at the proper time," Fargo said in a low voice. "I hope that works out here as well."

"We talking about Stonewall Jackson?" Gabriel said.

"Some called him that," Fargo said. After a moment, he asked, "Are we going to give Esparza an opportunity to surrender?"

"Absolutely not," Mariella said. "He should be shot on sight. He doesn't deserve any better."

"I'm a soldier, my dear, not a murderer," the general said. "If Esparza is willing to order his men to throw down their arms, we will accept his surrender."

Gabriel suspected it was a moot argument—Esparza wasn't going to throw down his arms.

They were too close for talking now. Gabriel and Fargo used hand signals to tell the people of Cuchatlán to spread out. The men armed with the machine pistols were posted at intervals along the line. The others had only the chunks of rock they had brought with them from the ruined palace, but those rocks could be deadly enough at close quarters, as they'd already demonstrated back on the steps.

After motioning for Cierra and Mariella to stay with them, Gabriel and Fargo looked at each other and exchanged a nod. They stepped up to the edge of the big circle of light cast around the Well of Eternity by the bright, generator-powered lights that had been set up.

For the first few seconds no one noticed them. That gave Gabriel a chance to take in the scene. A thick hose extended down into the Well and was attached to a pump. Hoses led from the pump to several metal barrels that were being filled by Esparza's men. Esparza, Podnemovitch, and the turncoat Hector stood beside the pump, watching the operation.

This was not a man to content himself with turning samples over to scientists—he was pumping water out by the barrelful, as fast as it would come. Mariella had said that the people of Cuchatlán had pack mules that had been trained to cross the rope bridge. Esparza had to be planning to pack the water barrels out by mule and then take them to wherever he had left his trucks. From there they could be taken back to Mexico City, where he could do with it as he pleased: analyze some, sell the rest, always setting enough aside, of course, to keep Esparza himself alive for centuries. That would be the plan anyway. What a laugh, when he discovered that, with the water's diminished potency, all these many barrels wouldn't buy him more than a few extra weeks or months of youth at most.

So why not let him take it? Because he'd surely kill the people of Cuchatlán before he left, and destroy the valley—and because there was always a chance, however slim, that his scientists would find a way to restore the water's potency. His were simply too dangerous a pair of hands to leave that power in.

Gabriel raised his voice and called out: "Esparza!"

Podnemovitch reacted first, spinning around and reaching for the revolver holstered on his hip. He stopped, with his lips twisting in a snarl, as he saw the guns aimed at him from every direction.

Esparza turned more deliberately. He glared at Gabriel and said, "Is there no end to your troublemaking, Hunt?"

"This is the end, sir," Fargo said, his deep voice booming. "I call upon you and your men to lay down your arms and cease hostilities. If you do, there will be no more killing."

"You think I fear a bunch of creaky old men?" Esparza shook his head. "You possessed the power to remake the world, and what did you do with it? Nothing! You hid here at the end of the earth like cowards!"

"We lived the lives we chose," Fargo replied, still holding his head high, his expression a model of pride and dignity.

"You disgust me," Esparza said. "Power is to be used, or it is nothing."

"Should we kill them, Vladimir?" Podnemovitch asked. The fact that Gabriel and the others had the drop on him and his allies seemed to mean nothing to him.

Esparza hesitated. If he gave the order to shoot, his men would open fire. But Esparza himself might be caught in the crossfire. He didn't want that.

Gabriel saw the doubt in the man's eyes and tried to tip the balance. If he thought there was no longer anything to fight for, he might be more inclined to surrender.

"Have you ever asked yourself, Esparza," Gabriel

said, "why everyone in Cuchatlán is starting to look so old?"

"They *are* old, Hunt. They're the oldest people on the planet."

"But they didn't used to look this old, Esparza. That's new. They explained it to me. The Well is wearing out. Its power is fading. The water doesn't work anymore."

Esparza's eyes widened as the implications of Gabriel's words soaked in. His head jerked toward Hector, and he snarled a curse.

"Did you know this, you worm?" Esparza said. "Is it true?"

Hector stammered, "I . . . I don't know . . ."

"You led me down here for nothing!"

Hector held his hands up and started to back away, saying, "No, señor, no! I . . . I swear, the water still has its power—"

Esparza yanked a knife from the sheath at his belt and shouted, "Kill them, Alexei! Kill them all!" as he lunged at Hector and plunged the blade into the traitor's belly. Hector screamed as the knife sank deep into his flesh.

"Fire!" Podnemovitch bellowed. He palmed out his revolver with one hand and reached behind his back with the other. That hand came into view holding Gabriel's Peacemaker. Both guns spurted flame.

Gabriel dropped to a knee and squeezed off a burst from the machine pistol he held. Fargo and the other men were shooting now, as was Cierra. So were Esparza's men. The night air, which just moments earlier had been so peaceful, was filled with the sudden thundering of guns and the whizzing of bullets. Up at the top of the palace steps, the machine gun kicked in as well, sending slugs ripping through the camp Esparza's men had set up.

Podnemovitch rolled away from Gabriel's shots. The

slugs stitched into the water barrels instead as Podnemovitch took cover behind them. Water began to spurt from the holes.

Esparza shouted in fury as he saw the water splashing on the ground—perhaps, Gabriel thought, he hadn't entirely accepted that the water had lost its power. Esparza jerked his pistol from the holster at his waist and fired at Gabriel and Fargo, forcing them to veer apart so that the bullets passed between them.

Fargo's gun jammed. He threw it aside, and at that moment one of his men came running up and held something out to him.

"General! We found it in the hut with the guns!"

Fargo wrapped his hand around the hilt of a cavalry saber. A smile appeared on his weathered old face. "My good friend," he said, and Gabriel wasn't sure if he was talking to the man who had brought him the saber—or to the blade itself.

With a chilling Rebel yell, Fargo lifted the saber and charged through the chaos toward Esparza.

Gabriel, meanwhile, went after Podnemovitch. Like Fargo, he'd already emptied his pistol, so he charged bodily into the barrels, sending them crashing against the Russian. Podnemovitch yelled as the barrels tumbled around him, knocking him over and dashing the guns from his fists.

Gabriel bounded over one of the barrels and tackled Podnemovitch as the man tried to get up. They rolled over and Gabriel realized they were just inches from the lip of the well. Podnemovitch wound up on top, and he managed to get his hands around Gabriel's neck.

"Here we are again," the Russian said, breathing heavily. "Just like in New York. I seem forever to be strangling you, Hunt. But this time—" he said, squeezing viciously "—I am going . . . to make it . . . *stick.*"

Gabriel had the fingers of one hand inside Podnemovitch's grip, and that was the only thing that had kept the Russian from crushing his larynx—so far.

The faces of the two men were only inches apart as the desperate struggle continued. Between gritted teeth, Podnemovitch said, "Do you want to know how my shoulder healed so fast after you bayoneted me, Hunt? Do you?" A harsh laugh came from him. "I drank the water that dog Hector brought to Mexico City! The water *does* work. I will live forever, you fool!"

Gabriel had been gathering his strength while Podnemovitch gloated. Now he acted, using all the power in his rangy body to arch himself up from the flagstones and plant a knee in Podnemovitch's belly. At the same time, he grabbed the collar of the Russian's shirt and heaved as hard as he could. With a startled yell, Podnemovitch went up and over Gabriel's head . . .

And into the Well of Eternity.

Gabriel rolled over onto his belly and gasped for breath as he heard the huge splash from the bottom of the well. He didn't know how deep it was, but with its smooth, slimy sides, Podnemovitch wouldn't be able to climb out. Unless—

Gabriel raced to the pump, struggled to detach the suction mechanism leading down into the Well. From far below, he heard Podnemovitch grab hold and slowly begin an ascent. He was climbing the hose.

"I'll kill you, Hunt," came the Russian's voice, echoing from deep within the Well.

Gabriel wrestled with the end of the hose that was connected to the pump, trying to unlatch it. The thing was firmly attached, and Podnemovitch's weight was making it impossible to loosen it.

"It won't take me long to climb out," the Russian taunted, *"and when I do, I will kill you most painfully."* And indeed his voice was louder, closer than it had been. It wouldn't take him long.

Gabriel searched the ground for anything he might be able to use. He saw a knife lying half in shadow and snatched it up, began using it to saw away at the hose. The damn thing was too thick to cut quickly.

"Just fifteen feet, Hunt," the Russian jeered. Then: *"Fourteen."*

Gabriel swept sweat from his forehead with the back of one hand while he kept sawing with the other. The surface of the hose was finally showing signs of stress as he ran the blade furiously across it, back and forth, pressing hard with each stroke. The material was starting to part, to separate, and as it did, the pressure of the water inside helped drive the cut open wider.

"Just five more feet, you son of a bitch," Podnemovitch called.

Then the hose split, with a popping sound. Water went gushing everywhere, and Gabriel heard the big Russian fall once more, bellowing as he plunged. The severed hose whipped through the air, then dropped into the Well.

"Now try to climb out," Gabriel muttered. "You son of a bitch."

Gabriel heard another sound, a quieter cry of pain, and turned. A few yards away, General Fargo was struggling with Esparza. The general had hold of Esparza's right wrist and was straining to keep the man's gun aimed away from him; at the same time, Esparza was twisting Fargo's right wrist so that the general couldn't use his cavalry saber. It was a stalemate . . . but one that Esparza was slowly winning. It was Fargo who'd let out the whimper of pain that Gabriel had heard.

Suddenly, with a wrenching twist, Esparza jerked his gun hand free and swung the pistol toward Fargo. The muzzle was almost touching the general's chest when flame spurted from it. Fargo rocked back as the bullet drove into his body.

"Granville!" Mariella screamed and ran toward him.

Fargo dropped his sword as he collapsed. Mariella scooped it up and slashed at Esparza, driving him back. He howled in pain as the blade cut across his face, laying his cheek open to the bone. Cursing, Esparza swung his gun around and fired twice, hitting Mariella both times in the chest. She staggered and fell, collapsing next to Fargo.

Gabriel surged to his feet and started for Esparza. He didn't have a gun, just the knife, but at the moment he didn't particularly care. He was prepared to kill the man with his bare hands if necessary.

Esparza fired again. The bullet ripped along Gabriel's side, spinning him around and dropping him to his knees. The wound wasn't bad—he could breathe, he didn't think he was bleeding too badly. But it had stopped him, and now Esparza had drawn a bead on him for a finishing shot.

Before Esparza could pull the trigger, though, Cierra let go with a burst of fire that chewed up the ground around his feet. Esparza turned and dashed away into the darkness.

Gabriel struggled to his feet, one hand clamped to his wounded side, aware that the shooting was dying out around him. He saw bodies scattered around the plaza, some Esparza's men, others wearing the rustic clothes of the Cuchatlán dwellers. He also saw the living, the few who remained standing. And those, thank God, included none of Esparza's men.

Gabriel saw Fargo's saber lying on the ground next to the general and Mariella. He picked it up, pausing just long enough to confirm the worst: Both of them were dead.

Before dying, Mariella had managed to reach out and take Fargo's hand. They lay there together, hands clasped in death, just like in their wedding photograph.

"Gabriel!" Cierra cried as he started toward the jungle. "What are you doing?"

He glanced back at her, saw that she appeared to be all right, and said, "Going after Esparza."

Then, clutching the saber, he ran in the direction Esparza had fled.

Chapter 24

Esparza didn't have much of a lead, and Gabriel could hear him crashing through the vegetation ahead. Normally, Gabriel was confident he could have overtaken Esparza fairly quickly, but desperation gave the man strength and speed he might not have had otherwise and Gabriel's wound slowed him down.

Where were the damn snakes and jaguars when you needed them, Gabriel thought. If Esparza ran into one of those predators, it would slow him down, maybe even finish him off.

It seemed that the only predator abroad in the jungle tonight, though, was man.

Cuchatlán fell far behind them. Gabriel's heart slugged in his chest, and his lungs struggled to draw in enough of the tropical air. Sweat drenched him. But he kept moving, kept following Esparza's ragged trail.

If Esparza reached the Blade of the Gods and made it across, he might be able to get back to the trucks. He had probably left some men there, and he might try to return with them to Cuchatlán and finish off the survivors. Even if he didn't do that tonight, he could flee back to Mexico City, put together another expedition, and start this unholy affair all over again. This had to end now.

Gabriel suddenly broke out of the clinging vegetation and found himself on the grassy verge at the edge of the gorge. Esparza was about a fourth of the way across the sagging rope bridge. Gabriel could see him plainly in the moonlight.

He dragged a deep breath into his body and then called, "Esparza!"

Out on the bridge, Esparza stopped and turned. He flung up his pistol and fired as Gabriel ducked aside. The bullet whipped past Gabriel's head and whined off into the jungle.

"You'll never make it, Esparza," Gabriel called.

"Why not?" the man demanded as he pointed the gun at Gabriel again. "Tell me why I will not return in triumph to Cuchatlán some other day?"

"Because earlier," Gabriel said, "I cut through all but one strand of one of these anchor ropes, remember?"

And with that, Gabriel swept General Fargo's saber up brought it slashing down, parting the last of the ropes.

Esparza cried out in terror and rage. He fired his gun but the shot went blindly overhead. The anchor rope, meanwhile, slapped through the air with a loud twang and the planks of the bridge clattered violently as they struck against one another. Esparza dropped the gun and grabbed for the guide rope with both hands, but his fingers slipped off it. He grabbed at the planks as they went out from under him. He screamed as splinters dug into his scrabbling hands, but he couldn't hold on.

Still screaming, Esparza plunged out of sight into the thick darkness that cloaked the gorge. Gabriel listened hard and heard the screams all the way down . . . and the ripe thud that ended them.

He stood there for a long moment, breathing heavily and resting his free hand on one of the bridge posts.

Then, still carrying General Fargo's saber, he turned and started back to Cuchatlán.

Chapter 25

Two weeks later, in the Hunt Foundation brownstone, Michael called Gabriel and Cierra into his office from the library adjacent to it. Cierra had spent quite a few hours in the library since arriving in New York, poring through all the relevant volumes of history and archaeology the foundation possessed.

The days following the battle had seen more tragedy, as the years inevitably caught up to the oldest survivors of Cuchatlán, no matter how much water they drank from the Well. The younger members of the lost city's population were still alive, but most now wore the look of octogenarians.

The general and Mariella had been laid to rest side by side on a small hill overlooking the valley. Cierra had led the survivors in a prayer while Gabriel stood to one side and watched.

The other dead had been buried as well, with headstones for the residents of Cuchatlán and unmarked graves for Esparza's men. Podnemovitch was one Gabriel had been particularly glad to see the last of. They'd found the big Russian floating facedown; he must have hit his head and been knocked unconscious the second time he fell. The waters of the Well of Eternity might once have held the secret of eternal life, but Podnemovitch had drowned just fine in them.

Leaving Cuchatlán had not been easy. It had required Gabriel to make two dangerous climbs on the sheer rock face of the gorge, one down and one up, the latter with the severed end of the rope bridge strapped to his shoulders. Fortunately the natives had supplied plenty of climbing gear—nothing modern or high-tech, but Gabriel preferred it that way. And the difficult climbs had been as good a way as any for Gabriel to focus his attention on something other than recent events. He didn't especially want to think about the ordeal Mariella had gone through, or the traumas Cierra had suffered, or the deaths of so many innocents, or the loss of a man unique in history like General Fargo. Not to mention the loss of the Fountain of Youth— the Well of Eternity, whatever.

Instead, he concentrated on the climbs. He was an experienced climber, but the Blade of the Gods would have challenged the best. He took it slow on the way down and slower still on the way back up, resting overnight at the bottom in between. The entire remaining population of the valley was waiting for him when he slowly, carefully put one hand, then the other, over the edge of the gorge. They helped pull him up, secured the bridge, lashed it with new ropes to the anchor posts. They tested it carefully several times with mules before any people dared to cross, and when it held up, they declared it sound. Cierra was a little nervous, but Gabriel walked behind her all the way, one hand at her waist.

An uncomfortable trek of a day and a half brought them to Esparza's trucks, one of which Gabriel was able to hotwire. From there to the nearest village was a day's drive, and from there a rickety bus took them to

Villahermosa. A public phone had made it possible for Gabriel to call Michael and the foundation's jet was there nine hours later.

Now, as Michael placed a manila envelope on the desk in front of him, he said to Gabriel and Cierra, "I've got the final report on those water samples you brought back."

"And?" Gabriel said.

"And there's nothing out of the ordinary about them." He fished out page after page, turned them so Gabriel and Cierra could read them. Not that they could understand the details—they weren't chemists. But the conclusions were clear enough. The scientists had run every test they could think of and concluded that what Gabriel and Cierra had brought back from the Well of Eternity was plain water. Clean, drinkable; no parasites or impurities; no unusual minerals or trace elements. It was clean enough that you could bottle it and sell it, and who knows, maybe you could make a buck or two doing so—some companies had done nicely peddling water from the world's remote rain forests. But there was nothing whatsoever about the water that would produce any unsual effect.

"I guess whatever mineral deposit gave the water its power must have finally been exhausted," Cierra said.

"If it ever existed," Gabriel said.

"What, now you don't believe?"

"I believe that was General Fargo; I believe he lived a century and more. We'll never know if it was the water that did it. Maybe it was something else down there."

"Well, whatever it was is gone now," Cierra said.

"If only Fargo had decided to reach out to us sooner," Gabriel said, "maybe we could have done something—"

"Or maybe someone like Esparza would have gotten

control of it. You don't know. Things could have turned out a lot worse."

"And on that note," Michael said. He opened a drawer in his desk and took out a small brown bottle with a cork stopper in it. "Here's the last of the samples you brought back," he said. He held it out to Gabriel. "The scientists didn't need it. The others were enough."

"What am I supposed to do with it?"

"I thought you might want it," Michael said.

"You just said it's an ordinary bottle of water. You can get one like it at any corner grocery store."

"Pour it out if you like," Michael said. "I just figured it should be your choice."

Grinning, Gabriel took the bottle and pulled the cork. "Or maybe we should pass it around and each take a little swig? Just in case? Nothing like a little eternal youth to spark up an evening."

Cierra shook her head. "No, thank you. I don't want anything more to do with the Well of Eternity."

"Michael?"

"Thanks, but no," Michael said.

Gabriel took a deep breath. "Well, then . . . bottoms up." He lifted the bottle to his mouth.

He stopped before it touched his lips, though, and sat there like that for a heartbeat before lowering it. "Hell with it," he said with a shake of his head. "If living and dying is good enough for the rest of mankind, I guess it's good enough for me, too."

He walked across to the potted ficus that stood in the corner of Michael's office and emptied the bottle into the soil at its base.

"Now," he said as he tossed the bottle back to his brother, "if you'll both come with me, I know a place where they serve some single malt scotch that'll make you *feel* like you'll live forever."

Gabriel led Michael and Cierra out of the office, closing the door behind them. The ficus was cast into shadow as the door swung shut.

Its leaves had never looked hardier or more resilient.

And now—

a sneak preview of

the next Gabriel Hunt adventure:

HUNT THROUGH THE CRADLE OF FEAR

"Go," Gabriel shouted, and he fired once more into the pack of men racing toward them. It was his last bullet and it found its mark, dropping a burly Magyar in a fringed vest before the man could take Gabriel's head off with a two-handed swing of his sword. The curved blade fell from the man's hand as he spun and collapsed; it slid along the stone floor until Gabriel stopped it with his foot. A scimitar, three feet from hilt to point if it was an inch, the steel tarnished but still deadly enough. Gabriel transferred his Colt to his left hand and scooped the sword up with his right. Unless they'd kept count, they didn't know the gun was out of bullets, so keeping it in view might still do some good.

"Go," he said again, shooting a glance over his shoulder toward the stone wall where Sheba crouched, clutching the shreds of her dress to her chest. "Now!"

"I can't just leave you—"

"I'll be right behind you."

"There are too many for you to fight alone!"

There were. But having to keep an eye on Sheba didn't make things any easier. Gabriel feinted with the sword, then smashed it broadside against the face of a squat, muscular man who'd stepped forward in an aikido stance. He planted a boot in the man's midsection and shoved, toppling him backward into one of his cohorts.

Gabriel took two rapid steps back, felt the stone of the low wall against his legs. Sheba was beside him. She'd made the mistake of glancing down and now looked terrified.

"Just grab hold and keep your eyes closed," Gabriel said. "And bend your knees when you land."

With trembling hands she reached up for the shuttle locked onto the metal cable overhead. The inch-wide metal strand descended at a steep angle from the turret above them to the treeline far below. She slid one wrist through each of the padded loops and took hold of the handgrips, releasing the lock. "Please," she whispered, "be care—"

Gabriel shoved her off the wall. Her screams echoed as gravity pulled her down along the cable, loud at first, then quieter and quieter still. In the distance they heard branches crack and foliage cushion a fall.

He smiled at the two men in front of him and the three more behind them. "All right now, boys, no one else needs to die. She's gone. You can't bring her back."

"On the contrary," came a voice from behind the pack of men, and then Gabriel heard the uneven triplets of Lajos DeGroet's step: slap, slap, click; slap, slap, click. The men parted to either side as the point of DeGroet's iron walking stick appeared between them. "We can and we will. This is no more than a temporary setback."

Gabriel leveled the Colt at DeGroet as the man limped forward. "You might as well put that away, Hunt, unless you plan to throw it at me. I know it's empty."

"How do you know that?" Gabriel said.

"Because you haven't shot me with it yet."

Gabriel considered that for a moment, then returned

the gun to his holster, snapped it shut. He kept the scimitar raised and ready to strike—but he didn't swing it. He had some skill with a blade, could even wield an unfamiliar one like this one with some hope of success, but only a fool would try to attack Lajos DeGroet with a sword. A suicidal fool.

"And how, Mr. Hunt, were you proposing to follow your young friend? I do not see a second shuttle on the line anywhere, and if you tried it bare-handed, your palms would be shredded within ten yards."

Without looking behind him, Gabriel climbed up onto the wall, edged over to where the cable ran. His feet were steady, but he was conscious of being only one accidental step away from a three hundred foot plunge. The wind whipped teasingly at his clothes, as though eager to sweep him over the edge.

With his free hand, he unlatched his belt buckle and yanked the belt free. He slung it over the cable, caught the free end as it dropped toward his hand.

"I see," DeGroet said. "Yes. Well. That might work, Mr. Hunt, I suppose, depending on what that belt of yours is made out of. But before you attempt it, you might want to look up."

"Why?" Gabriel said, looking up. He saw a man run up to the edge of the turret, holding in each hand one arm of a gigantic pair of diagonal cutters. He positioned its open blades on either side of the cable.

"*Akarja hogy most csináljam uram?*" the man called, and DeGroet nodded. The blades came together with a snap like the closing of an alligator's jaws. Gabriel let go of his belt just before the end of the cable came snaking past and whipped out into the distance. They could all hear it whistling as it fell and ringing each time it struck the rock face on the way down.

"Now," DeGroet said, "you will put down that weapon and get off the wall and turn yourself over to Mr. Molnar's custody." A bald, round-faced man stared viciously at him and cracked the knuckles on one hand with his other. "I don't promise that he'll treat you gently; you did just kill his brother, after all. But I promise you'll live. You're no use to me dead."

"What makes you think I'll be useful to you alive?" Gabriel said.

"You really don't have a choice, do you?" DeGroet said. He pointed to either side of him with his stick. The five men around him came in closer. Gabriel looked from man to man, from face to face. Molnar's showed the fiercest emotion, but all of them looked as though they'd be glad to tear him limb from limb.

"That's where you're wrong, Lajos," Gabriel said. "There's always another choice." He let the scimitar drop, turned, and hurled himself into space . . .

*DON'T MISS THE NEXT EXCITING
ADVENTURE OF GABRIEL HUNT!*

DAVID ROBBINS

Doomsday. The end of all things.
Dreaded by many, scoffed at by skeptics.
And now it has come to pass.

At a remote site in Minnesota, filmmaker Kurt
Carpenter has built a secure compound and invited
a select group of people to bunker down until the
worst is over. The world into which they reemerge
is like nothing they've ever seen. At first they think
they're the only ones left. But they soon find out
how wrong they are. In the wasteland of what used
to be America, their battle to survive is only just
beginning...

ENDWORLD

DOOMSDAY

ISBN 13: 978-0-8439-6232-1